In Those Days:
Through the Fire

The Anakim Chronicles
Book I: Part 1

by David Perry

David Perry

This book is dedicated to family and friends, too numerous to list here, in danger of leaving out anyone who encouraged me, assisted me by reading the earlier versions of this book, or who endured my endless, unfounded enthusiasm over plot outlines and plans for publishing.

Special thanks to the Chez Brett well-read-necks who have engaged in similar creative works, who never failed to inspire me to continue with my own.

The events in this book are historical fantasy; although real world figures will appear from time to time, this is entirely a work of fiction. The story unfolds in various time frames. Use the icons at the beginnings of the chapters to help you quickly determine when and where that chapter will take place.

ISBN number: 978-0-578-95976-4

Anything else that can withstand fire must be put through the fire, and then it will be clean.

Numbers 31:23

Part 1

Chapter 1

"Fucking Americans!" shouted Ahmed into the air as he watched the A-10 soar overhead and listened to the percussive vomiting of a nearby response. "Hey, asshole! You *missed* us! Are there more civilians over there you can slaughter?" This he shouted in Arabic as he swung open the back doors of an ancient white van and reached for a black camera case.

"Just look at that smoke!" Faruq exhaled as he stood nearby in disbelief. "I can't believe – how could they possibly not – ?"

Ahmed worked diligently and quickly, gathering together his lightweight gear, checking the battery, "Did you have any more tape up there, Faruq? Faruq?"

He peered around the van at his friend and coworker, scratching his bearded chin with his free hand, gazing over Faruq's shoulder at a belch of black, a thick blossom rising into the pale late-afternoon overcast sky.

"Just say it with me, buddy. Fucking Americans. I know that you do not enjoy profanity, brother, but surely these last few days would have given Mohammed, may peace be upon his name, cause to assign profane names to these jackals."

"Fucking Americans," muttered Faruq as he turned to look at Ahmed.

"See?" said Ahmed with a wink. He shut the back doors to the van and ensured they were locked. He checked every door handle in turn. "I hear many sirens but I do not see police or Guard ... do you?"

He motioned to the smoke with a slight nod and they both began heading across the barren parking lot toward the sidewalk. A block and a half ahead they could see the source of the smoke. It spilled from a hole in the wall of a concrete building that could have admitted an adult elephant. If the elephant had been willing, a zebra on its back would not have hit its head upon entry.

"Wait here for a second," Ahmed said as he balanced the camera on his right shoulder and put his eye up to the piece to find proper focus. Simultaneous explosions sounded softly from miles to the east and to the north of where they were standing, and in the distance they could yet observe several bombers beginning to arc to the left.

"Mister Bush, respectfully, you have missed some priceless Etruscan statues!" Faruq shouted skyward. "Come back and finish the job, Mr. President! We can never have enough widows and orphans! Who else will clean up this mess?"

"That's the spirit!" Ahmed chuckled. The chuckles came from the back of the throat, inches away from the lump that had formed in his chest, constricting the muscles in a way that only momentarily distracted him from the raw anger that had begun to manifest in a swath of red on his forehead.

"You know, I heard that there are animals escaping from the zoo. I'm glad we were not sent out to get footage of that. It would be hard to explain to Nissa that I could not come home right away because I was being pinned to the ground by a panicked jaguar."

"It is your fault for using that excuse before … you are, how would they say, the Sunni who cried 'jaguar'!" said Faruq, fighting tears in his eyes as he watched flames begin to engulf a section of the southern wall of the Baghdad Museum.

Ahmed continued to videotape the fire as they walked slowly up the sidewalk. He kept waiting to hear the wail of a fire engine, but it was understandable that there would not be assistance available for some time. Who was making the decisions on where to expend limited resources to try and minimize the overall damage to Baghdad? he wondered. Ahead one block, to the left, he heard a noisy vehicle backfire and race into their field of vision just as they were crossing an empty street.

A black truck screeched to a halt twenty feet beyond the rightmost pile of rubble that had been created by the partially collapsed wall. Faruq's instincts led him to hop quickly onto the sidewalk and ambled seven feet westward to the front of a branch of the Central Bank of Iraq, windows amazingly intact, out of sight of the truck. Ahmed, though not in great shape and hoisting a camera on his shoulder, agilely followed suit.

Just as Faruq began to register a siren that was distant but approaching, his ears were assaulted by a loud blast that shattered the window three feet from Ahmed and caused them both to buckle over. Faruq placed his hands over his ears and Ahmed did his best to cover his ears with left hand on one side, hard plastic on the other. A second blast resounded and struck terror in their chests, and without being able to see it they were both sure it had come from near the Museum.

"Give me the camera," Faruq said to Ahmed.

Ahmed looked up to Faruq, who walked over shards of glass to the corner of the bank and peered around north towards the Museum. Ahmed couldn't see any further damage to the building, but a white car had parked in front of the black truck, and at least five people in green uniforms were milling about, carrying weapons, looking every which direction *except* where Faruq stood, and he found himself unconsciously flipping the camera on again and trying to zoom in on the scene. He kept the lens pointed towards the back of the truck, just as two of the men were opening the doors.

"Did the Museum get hit again?" Ahmed asked loudly and Faruq stepped back behind the building and put a warning finger to his mouth, though now the sky was alive again with the noise of a plane engine and – yes – clearly sirens in the vicinity. One to the northwest and one to the south.

"They ... look ... like *soldiers* ...?" said Faruq as he turned back to look at the scene through the viewfinder and then lowered the camera, because his naked eye would surely present him with something less ludicrous than what the viewfinder had shown ... "And ... um ... two extremely obese women in large head-to-toe burqas ... ?"

Ahmed screwed up his face and came to a position behind Faruq, ignoring common sense and his gut instincts to flee and leaning right to see what Faruq was looking at. Faruq had brought the camera back up to capture the two black lumps that had emerged from the back of the truck and were awkwardly moving towards the cavernous, flame-filled hole. It was as if they were black bushes with no visible appendages, and the gaits suggested limps ... or shackled feet ... or extremely advanced age.

"Not Republican Guard," Ahmed said as an almost-afterthought. He had been focused on the men with the automatic rifles. It was surely interesting that the Arab men did not appear to be proper military, but he couldn't help be more intrigued by the mobile black-clothed masses.

5

One of those masses had its surface broken to produce a hand. As if disembodied, the hand poked out of a small aperture near a man's waist and then motioned back to a truck. By the time the hand had morphed into a pointer, the hand had risen to the 'soldier's' forehead, who followed the pointer to the back of the truck to follow some unhearable command. The hand disappeared back into the black.

"Should we call Tariq?" asked Faruq, attempting to press his large frame even closer to the bank's wall but maintain a clear shot of the proceedings. He was grateful that it was a gray, overcast day, and wondered if their luck would hold out much longer. Ahmed had already decided that an elephant-and-zebra-sized hole belching flames would surely command the attention of these people more than their mostly-hidden selves seventy yards away would.

"He'll see this soon enough. That is to say, Allah willing, if we survive this – how do they say? – shock and awe," Ahmed replied.

Two of the navy-green-clad men returned from the truck with fire extinguishers and approached the column of smoke. The men disappeared into the column, followed by first one, then the second, rotund black blob. The smoke swallowed another man, who they now perceived to be wearing some kind of gas mask, leaving the remaining two to stand outside the hole.

Ahmed nervously scanned the street to the left and to the right from where they stood, finding it as empty as most of the streets had been on their drive there. Just about everyone in Baghdad who had access to a basement was in said basement. This left very few people out and about, and only increased the curiosity burning in Ahmed to ascertain the identities of the men standing outside the Museum. And – suddenly – to ascertain the identity of the people approaching in a third vehicle along the same street that ran past the gigantic hole.

Faruq watched as one of the two men lifted his rifle and pointed it straight at the windshield of the jeep that had stopped momentarily thirty yards from them, barely visible from Faruq's poor perspective.

Faruq had little experience with guns and with men who casually waved them about, but could not mistake the meaning of the gesture. That is to say, that

6

although a thirty-foot-high accidental entrance into a partial inferno would be something to stop and take a look at, it was time for the gentleman driving the jeep to nod in appreciation and get lost. The jeep remained in place. Five long seconds later, it showed no sign of moving.

Another five seconds passed, and Faruq whispered out of the corner of his mouth, "Ahmed, my friend. I do not believe either of us has a gun, yes? So I do believe *this* is where we tell Tariq we were unable to find the Museum. Or get past the roadblocks. Or past the open shock-and-awe craters in our beloved Baghdad streets."

"I am inclined to agree with you," Ahmed said as he watched the second uniformed man raise his rifle and begin to walk towards the jeep. "What is the range of that rifle, do you think?"

"If we head back the way we came, we will be visible and exposed the entire way. We should head *that* way first and circle around to our – "

The second man dropped immediately following the short, sharp shock of a *pock*! *pock*! – and Faruq had no doubt that just beyond his field of vision someone had exited the rear of the jeep … or maybe even a fourth vehicle had shown up. A loud spitting emerged from the rifle of the other green-clad man as he dropped to the sidewalk and rolled towards the street, hoping (it seemed to Faruq) to put the front of the jeep between himself and whoever had shot his partner, while putting on the defensive anyone in the front seat of the jeep.

"Ahmed! I am *not* a brave man but I feel like I should get as much of this as I can! They are not going to look this way and see my lens – head west, then south … get to the van and swing it around to the front of the bank, and then you and I will return this tape to HQ and go home to our wives, yes?" fell out of Faruq's mouth. His camera remained on and implausibly still as he said this.

Ahmed could see nothing of the proceedings at this point, standing on broken glass to Faruq's left, looking at him with a pained gut-fear expression.

"Truly we are not paid well enough for this, yes?" Ahmed said as he walked slowly backwards, increasing his gait, beginning to run. He would turn the corner and head around the block counterclockwise to where the van was parked.

The entire run was well out of the sight of the Museum until he turned the final corner and found himself a block south of where Faruq stood, two blocks south of the Museum. He kept the parked van between him and that action, though at this point there was intermittent gunfire ... a loud siren ... the engine of an aircraft again ...

He moved around the side of the van and just let the cacophony wash over him, doing his level best not to let the sound cause his hands to tremble so violently he could not fit the key into its lock properly. As he did this, he returned his gaze to the flaming hole in the wall truly not far enough away, wondering at the sudden stop of gunfire.

A block past Faruq, Ahmed watched a black mass emerged from smoke. This mass had grown in bulk, and this appeared to be due to a large, bulging bag over an amorphous shoulder. There were two green-clad man covering the exit of the bulk, who seemed to be having some difficulty getting through the crevasse on the first floor to the sidewalk, over a pile of concrete and dust and twisted metal.

The mass was moving towards the black truck from which it had originally emerged, but something impeded its progress from behind. As Ahmed shut the door behind him and stuck the key in the ignition, he watched the outer surface of the mass shift upwards, the putative burqa clearly stuck on something sharp and exposing two legs (wearing pants?) beneath.

The engine turned over and Ahmed glanced over his right shoulder to see if he could make a U-turn and head back around the block clockwise to retrieve Faruq from his precarious roost. The way was clear and he turned back to see the second blob emerge from the smoky hole and step over rubble and black cloth towards the truck, carrying a large box that looked to be quite hefty, even from that vast distance.

Ahmed stepped on the gas and beat back southward, taking the first right and caring little if he'd been spotted from two blocks away. He kept his eyes open, paranoid that at any moment the streets would be full of vehicles from which many, many men with guns would emerge.

Two more right turns and he was on the block that contained many newly-broken windows – and Faruq as well. Faruq had turned to gaze back at the van with a look unlike Ahmed had ever seen on his friend's face. He pulled across the

8

median, stopped at the sidewalk twenty feet from Faruq, and motioned towards him. Faruq took a step forward away from the corner and the camera hung limply by his side. He looked like he didn't recognize Ahmed in the van. He looked like he didn't recognize what a van was.

He abruptly shook it off and ran towards the van, crossing in front and getting into the passenger's side. "MOVE!!!" he shouted as he climbed in. "Head back, Ahmed! Drive straight through the intersection and turn right at the next street and we need to get the hell OUT of here!"

Faruq put the camera back up to his eye, and as Ahmed looked at him, he realized Faruq's intent and hit the gas pedal with more force than he'd intended, leaning forward to give the camera a clear view past his head. They accelerated spastically and shot through the intersection.

A block later he turned right, and Faruq kept his eyes peeled past Ahmed looking to make sure nothing happening at the Museum was going to come their way. A few blocks south Faruq motioned for him to turn left. Any attempt by Ahmed to ask a question was shushed down with shushes that grew less insistent with each block they put between them and the Museum. Faruq lowered the camera to his lap, and Ahmed finally decided it was safe to move over to the side of the vehicleless street.

"Faruq?" he asked. It took a full ten pregnant seconds before Faruq stopped staring straight ahead, and he turned to look at Ahmed. "It's just not possible," he said. "It *isn't*. I ... we have to ..." And then his mouth just snapped shut again as he looked down at his camera, turning it over in his hand and staring intently at the device as if it might dissipate if he did not keep looking at it.

"It really isn't possible," he reiterated.

"Are you okay?" Ahmed asked, "Did they see you?"

"Probably," Faruq said. Ahmed's eyes leapt up to the rearview mirror, then to the left, to the right ... but he saw nothing, hearing only the engines of an A-10, a few distant sirens, low-level percussive thumps ... the street behind them was empty.

Chapter 2

Leph lowered his head to enter the chamber where Alisha sat in deep recline. Her eyes opened slowly and she turned to her right as Leph took a few tentative steps. He stopped halfway in his approach and smiled broadly at her, looking around the room. He found it unsurprisingly spartan. "Would you like some water?" he asked as he drew near a natural ledge near the foot of the bed and lifted a clay pitcher.

Alisha smiled in turn, nodded. "And how is my husband?" she asked softly, taking her time to reach full consciousness, her right hand moving up to rest on her stomach.

Husband. An old-fashioned word that Leph very rarely heard, these days.

Leph walked nine feet alongside the bed and held out a clay cup. Alisha took it gingerly and took a sip, setting the cup down on the natural ledge that encircled half of the round chamber. Next to the cup Leph spotted a stack of tablets barely legible by the light of the small candles set inside brass bowls along the ledge.

"He wishes he could be here, naturally," Leph replied, taking time to examine Alisha's face for signs of her mood, condition, thoughts. Her smile did not leave her face physically. There was little on the matter they could say, needed to say, so they enjoyed a silent minute of reacquainting themselves with each others' faces.

Leph reached down and gingerly took Alisha's hand in his. Her bottom lip trembled momentarily, but she quickly recovered from the momentary lapse of composure. "What are you reading?" he asked, nodding at the tablets by her side.

She smiled again. "Rapha tells me it's another narrative of the Israelites," she said. "Apparently he has quite a few friends down there." Their smiles went through a series of subtle changes, ranging from satisfaction to concern to whimsy to slight despair. Leph adopted an appropriate look of curiosity.

"What narrative would that be?" he asked.

"Apparently he engaged some of their priests in a discussion of their origins. Before Egypt. Before the Flood. Long, long, long ago."

"I'm not sure their grasp of long is as good as *our* grasp of long," Leph couldn't help saying.

"And yet here they come, hoping to reclaim what they perceive was once theirs," she said. She took a sip of water and winced slightly. Leph's smile returned to concern.

"Is everything all right?" Leph asked, glancing down at her stomach as if an external inspection would be of any help at all.

"According to Miriam, I'm not experiencing anything out of the ordinary. She gives me some powdered root that's supposed to make the nausea more bearable. I think it's the same powdered root she gave me when my leg muscles were sore," Alisha said, "though it wasn't clear whether I was meant to ingest the powder or make a poultice out of it."

"This is a critical time," Leph said plainly, though there was clearly no need to. He was generally able to suppress any and all negativity in his thoughts, but once again he could not help feeling jealous that childbirth seemed relatively free of complications for all other creatures of the Earth. Easier for the mice. Easier for the lions. Easier for the Israelites, for that matter.

Alisha took the top clay tablet off of the stack and searched its contents for a while. "Evidently it is simply our lot to suffer difficulty in bringing children into this world. My pain is meant to remind me of the distant past, of transgressions, of deeds done that cannot be undone …"

"Transgressions!" Leph exhaled with considerably more volume than he'd intended. His usually ordered thoughts began scattering and reverberating around his head, as always coming back to the thought of responsibility. Must it not be that those most capable of acting responsibly have more than a small obligation to do so?

"I have this memory …" began Alisha, turning again to gaze into Leph's eyes, reinitiating unspoken communication between them that complemented the words they chose to speak aloud. "I remember sitting on a rock outside of the gates of Negev as a young woman … no more than 28 or 29 … and you asked me what I knew of the story of Adam and Eve."

"And you are reading on these tablets the story of Adam and Eve," Leph said with the verbal equivalent of a wink.

"I *am*," she answered. The candles in the room flickered, sending shadows dancing up and down the length of her pale face.

"The Israelites see things *differently*, it seems," she said in a tone of understatement in which Alisha excelled, a tone that had always attracted elders to her, that had opened doors leading to longstanding debates. She was regarded as having a penetrating insight into their nature, as well as into human nature.

Leph left her side temporarily and procured a wooden chair from the other side of the room, positioning himself near her bulging abdomen, reclining and getting comfortable.

"Would you indulge me, Leph? Would you tell me the story that you related to that girl many years ago on the outskirts of Negev?"

Outside of the chamber there was the occasional passerby. There were other caretakers making their rounds, visiting the reclining women in the neighboring chambers. More chambers, Leph gave unbidden thanks to Baal, than those containing injured comrades.

Janis – who had returned with him – having his broken arm set in place with rope and strong cords of wood. Makkid, who had had his side pierced by a dull iron blade that had caused him great pain and in recent days, persistent fever.

"You wish to hear of *Eden*," he said, taking her hand into his again. She nodded. He nodded slowly, understanding that she knew the story of Eden to be one of his cherished histories, the story to which he had devoted decades of meditation, on which he had sought out others' opinions, upon which he was filling clay tablets with ruminations, theories, tentative conclusions …

"Child, you are placing a skinned tuna fish at the front paws of a kitten and asking it kindly if it would enjoy taking a bite or two. Do you think that pontification in the guise of storytelling is a better cure for nausea than birch powder?"

"Your words are a *balm*, Leph. I need distraction from my husband's absence," Alisha said, and Leph once more enjoyed the nuances in her use of the word *husband*, which did not mean precisely the same thing as what *husband* meant to the Israelites, or to the other peoples about the globe.

"Tell me again about the Nephilim, Leph. Explain again the wrath of Yahweh. The love of Michael. Tell me again about Seth and Abel on Ararat. About Seth and Ada's final conversation, in her twilight …"

Given the scope of the random phrases she listed, and others unspoken, it was clear to Leph that there would be many changes of candles as they spoke, many shared meals, and outside of these walls the sun would rise and set a few times. Which would be nothing out of the ordinary.

"And where do you want me to start?" he asked, shifting slightly on the wooden chair to find a position that would keep him comfortable for the next seven hours.

It seemed fairly obvious to her, and obvious things would ordinarily be exchanged nonverbally between their kind. Nonetheless, she stroked her stomach thoughtfully and said, "In the *beginning*, of course."

Chapter 3

"Close your eyes and imagine their arrival. The closer they were to the Trees, the greener and lusher and denser and more *alive* the surroundings would have been. The direct approach from a mere mile away would likely have taken half a day, and no one undertook that approach immediately. It was enough to be *close* to the Trees. Even within a radius of 100 miles, one would have correctly felt that they had found themselves in Eden."

Leph did not actually use the word 'miles', as it was not how he measured distance, and he was not speaking in English.

"*Correctly* felt," Alisha murmured sleepily, closing her eyes and letting Leph's description enter her mind slowly, seeping past critical, conscious thought. An unseen grin appeared on his face. It would be the single, gentle admonishment showing that she understood the nature of the story and the nature of *truth*, and was happy to likewise close her eyes *metaphorically* for the time being.

"You and I have walked through forests in Lebanon so achingly beautiful they nearly brought a tear to the eye, and yet I am ... confident ... that *this* forest was more pristine and vibrant and ... well, *holy*," Leph said with a laugh at the obviousness of the adjective. "Noisy, too, with every manner of creature crawling and prowling and flying and climbing.

"It would be inaccurate to say they came out of curiosity. That comes later in the story, when the humans embraced and realized the *potential* of curiosity. At this point in time they were mostly afraid. And hungry. And greedy. And sometimes tender. To which they presumably never gave much thought. There are things no one of us would or *could* give thought to until some modicum of safety and comfort has been achieved, and perhaps their coming to Eden was an instinctual movement towards this elusive safety and comfort.

"Jophet led one group of humans into a glade where a stream offered them protection and water, and many fruit-producing trees were in the area, grapes growing wild, and most of the larger predators made their home well downstream.

"They had killed lions before during their travels and had lost two of their tribe during those attacks. They had developed sharp weapons and strategies, and increasingly understood that what *they* possessed that the lions did *not* possess would ultimately give them dominion over the lions, and indeed, over all of the creatures of the world.

"Lions are certainly clever in their pursuit of food, but humans even more so. Humans *made* things, and humans transformed growls, howls and screeches into meaning, developing syntax and abstractions for objects not present in their hands but present in their conversations.

"Mirab could stand on the flat rock in the middle of a gathering and relate the last encounter with the lions in Sinai, relate the brave deeds of Siroc, and she would *become* a lion though she was not-lion and everyone understood and sat transfixed, and she could tell the story again every several months and emotions would swell in their chests and their eyes would grow wide time after time after time …

"So we can readily understand what it must have seemed to them that twilight evening a lion padded its way toward the fire, toward the gathered humans.

"Jophet stood up swiftly and was checked by sudden paralysis. They must *all* have felt the instinct to grab their weapons and defend themselves, but none of them made a move to do so. It was a different kind of fear that kept them in place, and they could not even *begin* to express what made this new fear unique, but it must have had something to do with the manner in which the lion approached them, a lion unlike any lion that they had ever encountered.

"This lion appeared to be nearly twice as large as they had seen lions to be, and what appeared to be a trick of moon reflecting off the coat of the lion – even without a visible moon in the sky. They felt terror that was not-terror, and perhaps Mirab spent the next week thinking on the encounter and how it made her feel, and what thoughts entered her mind thereby, and she added the word *awe* to her vocabulary … to *their* vocabulary …

"'Why are you here?' Jophet found himself asking and was struck with the absurd ease with which the question left his mouth. To address a *lion*. Whereas his previous encounter with a lion involved cries and shouts coming from his mouth, and thrusts of a spear to wound the animal, to either kill it or to drive it away. It had not for a second occurred him to say, 'Would you mind terribly not eating us and simply go away?'

"And although they had already begun to find humor in living and discovered laughter to be an involuntary response to events and words that seemed to instinctually warrant the response, there was not a single human being who laughed when Jophet spoke to the lion. Why did that appear to be natural?

"The lion opened its mouth and made a low growl. It closed its mouth. It opened it and made a breath sound that turned into a whine that sounded like a poor attempt to yawn and sing at the same time. It padded up to where a woman sat, unable to move or breathe, feeling fear but having no expectation to die, trembling without understanding.

"The lion sniffed the woman's head and made a survey of the gathering, taking time to look at each one in turn. It padded its way back away from the fire and turned to watch the circle of humans again. Spears at the sides of most men remained untouched by any hand. It turned away again and padded its way into the forest, followed the stream a-ways, and eventually the glow of the lion faded completely into the dark."

Leph was silent for a while and Alisha opened her eyes slowly. "You never told me this part about the lion before," she said, feeling like she knew how it fit into the familiar story but enjoying not being certain. "This lion was the first of the Nephilim to greet them?" she asked.

Leph returned her smile and bowed his head slightly.

Chapter 4

Faruq's hands were shaking as he held the videotape in front of him, the passage of twenty minutes enough to make him doubt what he had actually witnessed, wondering if the videotape would establish that he had simply lost his mind back at the Baghdad Museum.

"Where is Tariq?" Faruq exhaled loudly. Ahmed stood in the doorway of the control room and turned to look down the corridor, seeing no one approach.

"He is no doubt chatting up the talent," Ahmed replied, "The newsreader that arrived yesterday is indeed quite attractive, and he would be unwise to shuck the cad's prerogative to try and coax Fatima into surrendering her virtue during this *trying* time of unprovoked American aggression …"

"This really can't wait," Faruq said with an uncharacteristic quaver.

Ahmed looked at his friend with concern. They had seen their share of horrific violence and injured children and sheer inhumanity, and he was beginning to steel himself against whatever Faruq had captured on the tape while he had gone to retrieve the van. "You have to see what was under the burqa."

"One of the fat women's burqas came *off?*" Ahmed said in a rude chortling tone he was immediately embarrassed by.

"One of the burqas got caught on a piece of debris outside of the hole in the side of the Museum …" Faruq said carefully as he gingerly pushed the tape into a VCR and pressed play.

He took a quick survey of the series of buttons and controls on the panel in front of him and stared pensively at a single button that stood at the very edge of the panel.

While footage of their northward progress along the sidewalk played on a large screen before them, he pressed the button casually and sighed, adding, "It was not a woman under the burqa." He turned to Ahmed with a look of inarticulable distress.

"There was a *man* underneath the burqa?!" exploded from Ahmed's mouth, and at this point, he moved slightly in front of the seated Faruq and grabbed the control to fast-forwarded the video, stopping at the point when the two black masses were entering the hole. He returned the video to normal speed to more deliberately watch them walk the sidewalk accompanied by escorts.

The level of zoom allowed him to see the unlikely parade in much finer detail than he had in person. "*Saddam!?*"

"It was not a man under the burqa," Faruq said soberly as he sunk into a chair, wheeling it backwards, allowing Ahmed easier access.

Ahmed hit the pause button, and stared intently at the black masses. It was not helpful that the flames behind the masses only served to mask the lines along the fabric that would have given any indication of the shape underneath, though his initial impression that there was something wrong with the way the closer mass moved was borne out when he hit play again to watch the scene unfold.

"And why did you just say this ridiculous thing?" Tariq asked upon entering the room, just in time to see the second burqa-clad mass step through the hole in the wall, followed by a man in a gas mask holding a fire extinguisher.

Tariq was in his mid-twenties, barely coming up to Ahmed's shoulders, thin with a Sharif mustache that came just shy of being an asset, and only served to make him seem like the clothes he was wearing were two sizes too large for him. His high-pitched voice and affected stance of importance helped everyone around him feel guiltless in not taking him seriously.

"Why would there be a man under that burqa? And such a *fat* man at that?"

Faruq swiveled in his chair as the two remaining men in navy green took up positions on either side of the fiery gash in the wall.

"*Big* … not *fat* …" Faruq said, "And please, can we just watch what's on the tape so I don't have to try and explain any further? I'm no longer even sure of what I saw. Maybe I was just in shock from …"

The first spate of bullets sounded tinny and surreal coming out of the speakers. All faces snapped to attention and they sat silently as the rest of the action unfolded.

The camera panned to the left to capture the front of the jeep, only partially visible because of the bank and other buildings along that block. After being challenged to leave, someone had clearly emerged from the jeep and was firing at the two guards, dropping one immediately and forcing the other to roll into the street to return fire. After the roll and return fire, the guard got to his feet and made his way towards the jeep, kneeling down to replace the clip in his rifle.

One of the other uniformed men emerged from the hole then. The black smoke must have given him a poor view of the outside, as he was clearly surprised by the sight of his comrade lying on the ground in a growing pool of blood.

The man was carrying a small metal chest and wore a gas mask. With surprising efficiency that bespoke experience, the emerger leapt over his comrade's body into a half-kneel, setting down the chest and bringing up the pistol clipped to his side, and immediately fired twice at targets the camera had yet to capture.

Faruq imagined that it came as a relief to the fellow in distress closer to the jeep, who turned and made a series of hand motions that presumably gave some notion as to the locations and numbers of attackers.

A second man in green emerged from the hole, made a putative quick assessment of the situation and joined the other two men in the assault on the unexpected (?) company.

A black mass emerged from the hole, carrying a large sack over the shoulder. It was clearly heavy, as the mass appeared acutely awkward in its movements. The black cloth wrapping the looter – who was clearly removing something from the Museum – scraped against stray brick, concrete, and broken, twisted metal rods, impeding the mass's progress until it became stuck *fast*.

The mass was yanked back, held in place, cloth lifted, exposing for the first time a set of large feet in boots underneath. *Enormous* feet, it appeared to the three watching the tape.

19

At this point the frame centered on the struggling figure, so most of the action was now off-screen, yet clearly audible. The more they could hear gunfire, it was clear that something was still unfolding, and the sound of approaching sirens and a plane overhead made the three of them tense.

Tariq came up to the controls and hit the pause button and cocked his head to the side.

He had been right in assessing that an exceptionally loud aircraft was at that precise moment flying over the Baghdad Headquarters of Al Jazeera. For the sound to have reached them where they were in the building, it had to have been exceptionally close, and all three felt relief when the sound stopped crescendoing and began descrescendoing.

Faruq looked up at the two. "It happens really soon," he said, "The burqa comes off soon."

"Is it too much to hope that she is wearing only those boots and weighs no more than 300 pounds?" Tariq asked with raised eyebrows that made Faruq's nausea flare and subside, leaving the unpleasant taste of bile in his mouth.

"As I explained to Ahmed before, it is not a woman under the burqa," he said softly.

"No, no – I heard you say that it was not a *man* under the burqa," Tariq began.

"Shut *up!*" Faruq said impatiently, stood to forcefully hit the play button, returned to his seat. Tariq shot him an angry look before realizing that Faruq had not and would not acknowledge it.

At the end of a long struggle to get free of a particularly complicated snagging situation, the burqa on the mass did come entirely off, and what appeared to be a black-uniformed man emerged from the bulk of cloth, temporarily letting the heavy bag go, clearly with the intent of getting untangled before retrieving whatever had been removed from the Museum.

Once again Tariq stabbed at the pause button and asked incredulously, "In what universe is that *not* a man?!"

With turned head, the men before the screen took in a distinguished, handsome face with dark complexion and a mustache and beard Tariq immediately envied – the gaze of this man was back towards the rubble on the ground, the flames beyond that, taking in some desperate battle unfolding offscreen, thirty yards or so further.

Tariq happened to look down to see a flashing red light above the button at the very edge of the control board Faruq had pressed ten minutes earlier. "You're sending this to *Qatar*? Before I had even *seen* it? Before we've edited it in any manner?"

"I'm trying to send this to Qatar, but you keep pausing the feed," Faruq said wearily. "And I agree with you that you appear to be looking at a man there who has freed himself from a heavy burden and an awkward-fitting burqa. But you are forgetting that I have zoomed in fully on the figure. Will you *please* just watch the next twenty seconds of the video?"

Tariq was not used to Faruq raising his voice to him. Faruq was a sober man who was unwaveringly polite and usually mindful of who was signing his paychecks. Although Tariq was not an exceptionally introspective person, he stepped outside of himself long enough to decide that perhaps he should stop hitting the pause button and hold all discussion until the end of the tape.

Tariq pressed play.

The camera zoomed out slightly and captured the man standing erect as the other (and now sole) black mass entered the left side of the frame, stooped over, scrabbling ahead in an awkward gait.

As the second mass put down a sack and bent down to free the snagged burqa from a twisted metal bar that had been part of the wall, a uniformed man entered from the left-hand side of the screen, stopping to stand next to them. This action took place as the camera zoomed out, and shadowy blobs snapped back into focus.

Ahmed and Tariq both gasped and resisted the temptation to hit the pause button again. Standing erect, the 'man' who had emerged from underneath the burqa stood at least four feet taller than the man in the uniform, who positioned himself as a shield against the forces off the screen, and continued firing his rifle towards the left side of the screen.

The rifle was lowered, and no more sign of gunfire could be heard.

The rest of the scene showed a rapid evacuation, green-clad man and burqa-mass and – a *giant* man – loading bags and injured parties into the black truck that had first arrived at the Museum.

The jeep on the left lurched forward and shot past the truck – driven by one of the men in a green uniform, which Faruq took as a sign that every single interloper had all been dropped, would be left behind. An approaching siren grew louder, but the source of the siren was never seen.

The tape ended abruptly in static.

"That's impossible," Tariq said. "When that … *man* … was loading the semi, he was almost as tall as …"

"The *truck*," Ahmed finished, stroking his beard and letting out a forceful sigh that was the last sound any of them made for the next thirty seconds.

Chapter 5

Saul's army had settled in the Valley of Elah three weeks earlier.

Saul sat in his tent with eyes closed, breathing in deeply the slightly salty air borne by a westerly wind over Lake Asphaltitus, a lake so suffused with salt that it could not bear life. What it *could* do, however, was provide salt to his cooks, and he anticipated a modest meal of lamb and unleavened bread coming within the hour.

Jesse entered the tent bearing a crude oil lamp, illuminating the living quarters of his master, his commander, the leader of the Israelites.

"Is there anything you require before your evening meal?" he asked, bowing slightly and standing attentively. Saul turned from his seat to regard Jesse – hair thin, just shy of gray – well-regarded by those who had known him in Bethlehem, a self-made man whose family now maintained the flock that, among other things, provided daily sustenance for the current campaign.

"Have a seat, Jesse," he said, motioning to a short wooden stool at his side. Spread out on the table was a crude dried gazelle skin with colorful pigments marking out bodies of water, mountains, names of cities currently ruled or inhabited by the Israelites, alongside those that belonged to the Philistines and to the Anakim. "And how is your family?"

"We are all quite well, your highness," said Jesse, "Abinadab is very eager to enter the fray. Out of all my sons it is perhaps he who sees most clearly the need to carry out this campaign to its bitter conclusion."

"Please," said Saul with a dismissive gesture, "Dispense with the title. This is a shared mission between all of us who follow Yahweh and the commandments made to Moses ..." A fragment of the last hour of contemplation was pouring out of his mouth.

"Brought to this land once again by the sword of Joshua ..." He smiled briefly, inhaled deeply, and allowed, "I guess I *sound* like the title ... apologies, friend ... I'm glad to hear that Abinadab is prepared. We will break camp and approach Sokoh two days from now."

"I regret I cannot spare you more of my sons to begin the siege," Jesse said, "Though truth be told, the youngest are probably better suited to tending our family's sheep … some of which are being prepared as we speak, and I will bring you your meal shortly."

"If you could, bring several meals here … I believe that Abner will be busy with preparations but I anticipate that Jonathon and Michal will be joining me tonight."

"Michal is *here*? In this *camp*?" Jesse asked with surprise.

"Obviously I will be sending her back to Bethlehem in the morning," Saul said, "But she has it in her mind to watch our preparations unfold … and I am beginning to wonder if perhaps Michal is more interested in the watching the actions of *Shammah* unfold." Jesse blanched a little.

"Do you *think*? I'm not sure I have seen Shammah and Michal together …"

Jonathon entered the tent carrying a skin full of water, set down a spear and a sling, walked over to stand across the short table from where Jesse and Saul were seated.

"Father, I have exceptional news," Jonathon said excitedly, "We've received word from our ears in Sokoh." He spoke with much animation, making up for his lack of stature with forceful hand gestures, sounding out of breath from excitement, not exertion, and Saul regarded him somewhat neutrally. While he waited for Saul to finish a protracted visual inspection of his person, Michal entered the tent behind him.

Michal wore a simple dress made of gray wool, with a messy swath of twine keeping her long, black, curly hair from spilling over her shoulders in haphazard splay. She approached the table and positioned herself between Jonathon and the seated Jesse, saying nothing as she nodded to each in turn.

"Michal, we need to discuss the campaign," Saul said flatly. Michal said nothing, meeting his gaze and holding it for the next ten seconds before she spoke. She made no move to quit the tent.

"Father, there are 3,460 foot soldiers here in the camp of Elah. Nearly all are armed with spears and we have been able to manufacture nearly four times as many arrows as there are men, so only a *fifth* of the men will serve as bowmen, laying cover for the moment in which the siege turns into a battle."

Took a breath.

"Sokoh is a walled city but it is an *Anakim* city and they did not build it to secure it from invasion, but rather to keep most animals from simply entering and milling about their wide avenues ..."

Saul raised his hand and she closed her lips into the not-a-smile smile that had gotten her out of punishment when she had been caught stealing honey straight from a clay jar in her youth. "Jonathon, please give us the report from Sokoh," he said.

Jonathon peered a little nervously at Michal, five years younger and a more natural speaker. She had an ease about her that twenty-seven years had yet to afford him a fraction of, but there was simply no alternative. As eldest of Saul's children, he would of necessity *manufacture* the ease and the poise that Michal had inherited from Saul and from their mother.

"There is broad talk that the Anakim are finished with this world. There is talk that they will not follow Baal into this battle," he began, and Saul raised his eyebrows.

"I do not believe – " erupted from Michal's lips, and she immediately stopped short and berated herself internally. "I'm sorry, Jonathon. Please continue."

Jonathon fought displaying any external sign of alarm and annoyance, but felt a red-hot cheek eruption, as if Michal had grasped his robe firmly at his shoulders and brought it down, undergarments included, into a pool at his feet in front of his regiment.

He cleared his throat, as the mental image had caused something inexpressible to flit through his mind. He looked over at Michal and found red in her cheeks as well, and the anger he was feeling subsided. Perhaps he loved Michal more than anything else in this world.

"It is rumored that the vast majority of the Anakim have gone east. And although we had assumed that they were intending to settle among the Zamzummims on the left bank of the Tigris, there is word that in fact the Zamzummims are joining *them*, together abandoning the lands of Yahweh and Baal and traveling further east, to lands mostly unknown to us," he said.

"Why make this stand in Sokoh, if they are leaving?" Saul asked. Earlier reports had indicated that they were reinforcing the city while Saul's army kept camp just a few leagues to the south.

For Saul, this was just one stop on an extended campaign meant to drive the Anakim further and further north and east, removing this abomination from the lands that were rightfully theirs, removing the Anakim from *all* lands – *if* the Israelites remained faithful and Yahweh saw fit to reward them.

"But why not move the fight to Jerusalem? Why make their last stand in Sokoh?"

"Only the *Anakim* are making their last stand in Sokoh," Jonathon replied, "The Philistines and other worshippers of Baal will no doubt expend many lives and many years trying to keep the Israelites from reclaiming *all* lands of Canaan."

"I cannot even *begin* to fathom what goes through the minds of the Anakim," Jonathon admitted, "I do not understand why three centuries ago they did not emerge from Jericho and lay waste to the army of Joshua rather than letting the city fall. They must simply fear Yahweh because it is hard to imagine they fear … well, you know … *us* …"

Jonathon was once again interrupted, but this time it was by a whirlwind that burst through the tent entrance, screaming, "Is my father in here? Father, are you *here*?"

The whirlwind froze in place, not expecting to see any kind of crowd, but there was clearly a group of men around a table in deep discussion, given their annoyed looks.

Jonathon stood to the left of the table – aside someone with their back turned to him – his father and Saul sitting at the table on the right. His father stood up so abruptly the chair behind him became airborne for a second, tumbling away from him and into the side of the tent, nearly taking out a stand bearing a small oil lamp.

"DAVID!" Jesse shouted, "Get out of here right now!"

"But father! There is an emergency at home ... the sheep ..." had fallen out of his mouth before his throat constricted in response to the onslaught of fury in his father's eyes, stronger perhaps than he had ever seen therein.

"The *SHEEP?!*" Jesse spat, his hands grasping at his waist as if looking to find a sturdy club there, or a spear, but those days were long past him. Saul was actually amused and put a warning hand on Jesse's forearm.

If something was wrong with the sheep, and dinner would not come the next day or the next, then this perhaps *was* an emergency.

David could not seem to find his words, and just when he was about to, the fourth person in the tent, made nearly invisible by the bright light of the lamp behind him ... no, not him ... *her* ... turned to regard David.

Whatever he had just found the courage to say dissipated in a heartbeat, and would not return for many heartbeats. And then her eyes took *possession* of his heartbeats, possession of the words that began careening around his skull, words that wanted to express how captivating were those dark eyes, those full lips, and for the love of Yahweh was there a single tendril of curly hair making its way past her right cheek as she tilted her head and began to smile at what *surely* must have been a *pathetic* sight?

"I ..." David stammered, suddenly finding a reserve of courage he had never known he possessed. "I will take *care* of it, Father." He bowed low and forced himself to look only towards Saul and his father when he brought his head back up. *"Somehow."*

And a bead of sweat was already forming on his forehead. And two seconds later he had departed from the tent, and Michal found herself watching the flap of the tent sway, then cease to sway.

"David will tend to the sheep and Shammah will tend to the Anakim," Saul said with some amusement, and Jesse felt his wrath begin to disappear. "And David will become a fine soldier *someday*."

Jonathon's eyes had turned cold, but by the time Michal turned back towards him, the coldness had retreated behind a well-maintained wall.

Chapter 6

Jophet and his large tribe of followers made their way along a stream – which became a river – and they followed the river simply because it felt right to. They would make camp every evening and would build a fire, roasting the small animals they had killed during the day.

Often this included fish, as Mehujael had invented a means of taking a number of fallen tree parts riddled with branchlets and interlacing them into a barrier that large fish could not pass through, nor avoid when the current was sufficiently rapid. Trial and error had taught Mehujael that a swift pull of his apparatus while a fish struggled would usually cause the fish to fly shoreward and into gourd shells held by his agile partners.

Mirab had already been relating the story of the recent encounter with the lion during their evening rituals, which had taken place four days earlier. She would pad about the camp and approach children and snuffle at their hair, just as the gigantic lion had snuffled the hair of Lilith on that day.

Siroc would lead a contingent of the men in exercises, though attacks from animals near the river occurred less frequently than whence they had traveled. Although filled with a feeling of increased safety, Siroc would not allow the men to cease exercising, and Jophet did not allow the tribe to cease the activities that supported Siroc's men.

One morning the tribe broke camp again and continued to move along the river. The grass was increasingly thick, the trees in tighter formations, and all manner of insects buzzed and flitted and bit, though there was an ointment made out of animal fat and the secretions of a particular tree that seemed to bring relief from most hungry bugs.

By mid-afternoon it was time to camp anew and prepare food for the evening meal. They had enough meat from the previous day, and there were at least three different varieties of fruit-bearing trees that were safe to eat. It was not long before evening began to fall and a fire was built, and people huddled together for warmth.

Mirab and her friend Zillah prepared to reenact the slaying of a bear that had occurred nearly a year earlier, when noise of the approach of something large began to attract the attention of everyone, eyes moving in all directions to ascertain the source. It was young Carmi who first spotted the glow, and then others spotted the glow, and the glow was the same color that had come from the lion five days earlier.

This time Siroc did pick up his spear, though every muscle in his arm he needed to *strain* to flex. He could not dismiss the feeling of calm that was somehow being thrust upon him, *into* him, and it was this sourceless thrust that allowed him to maintain a mustard seed of resolve, and to nurse it into continual life.

Three hundred yards away – then two hundred. Eighty. Thirty yards from their small clearing, branches and brush were swept away by two arms and the opened greenery revealed a glowing figure that stood on two legs, not four, and this figure was naked and unashamed and walked with purpose directly towards their assembly.

Every one of them felt a slight vertigo of perception. They could not seem to gauge the distance between this man and where they sat, and suddenly the man appeared before them, though he had seemed twenty feet away a second earlier.

With his feet planted at the edge of the gathering, Mehujael stood up and walked five feet to stand next to the arrived person, craning his neck and looking skyward, as this entity turned downward to meet his gaze. With an abrupt start, Mehujael backed off two feet to avoid touching the man's private parts with his chin, as the head of this man was another six feet off of the ground from where Mehujael's eyes peered upward.

"WHY ARE YOU HERE?" bellowed the man. No, thought Jophet – *not* a man.

Almost as one, the humans rose to their feet, and each and every man, woman, and child marveled at how little difference it made to the sight before their eyes when they stood up. This – *being* – before them was twice as tall as their tallest.

"Why are we here?" Jophet repeated the question, remembering suddenly that this had been the question he had last posed to the lion that had glowed in the precise same manner. It was the kind of question that he had to pause and spend time finding the right words to respond to, much like every other question posed by Mehujael.

"We are simply traveling together, finding food and water where we can." No one, not even Mehujael, could think of a more complete response. Indeed, a few of them were too young to remember Mehujael even adding the word 'why' to their vocabulary. They understood hunger and pain and shouting in alarm. They had for many years lived in a world where there was not a lot of use for 'why'.

"Where are you going?" asked the gigantic being, who had seemingly understood that the physical apparati he was manipulating to create these sounds could be controlled with what he knew to be his diaphragm, echoing more closely the volume emerging from these humans.

Jophet bent his head slightly at this question. But it was an easier question to answer. He pointed to the river and moved his hand left along its bank. "Up this river," he said, "to its *source*."

The glowing man adopted an indecipherable look upon its face and simply asked, "Why?"

Jophet's eyes narrowed, feeling slightly weak at the knees and feeling bees buzzing throughout his skull. Although a gifted leader, Jophet found himself lacking confidence and felt discomfort of a nature that he had never before experienced.

"I do not understand why," he said slowly, and could not find any trace of a better response in the quizzical faces of his tribemates. Inside his head he heard a voice that sounded like his own ask, 'Why *are* you going up this river to its source?' – and wondering at the answer – and wondering about wondering. He began to feel ill.

"I am uncertain whether or not I can allow you to proceed along this river," the giant man mused, and Siroc felt his hand tighten about his spear, and suddenly Jophet could feel emotions he was *quite* familiar with.

Allow. Permit. Restrict.

He could feel a thin red line slicing through a sense of calm from a source he *still* could not identify, and therefore could not trust. He had lived enough years and had killed enough things to understand that he should *not* be feeling calm.

31

Chapter 7

"Three meters ... three and a half ..." Tariq mumbled.

"Four, *maybe* ... a little less than twice the height of the men in green uniforms," Ahmed said, pointing towards the screen, the video paused at the moment when the burqa-clad stooped giants were exiting the back of the truck. Ahmed fast-forwarded the video twelve to thirteen minutes ahead and paused again when the derobed giant stood behind the open doors, using the top of one to balance himself as he got in.

For a moment, Tariq's mind flashed to the scene in *Jurassic Park* where a man enters the jaws of a Tyrannosaurus Rex, which he had watched the night before with his two boys, and marveled at how real it had looked. Tariq was alone in indulging such a thought – the other two were as pale as their melanin-infused skins allowed.

"Okay, okay," Faruq said as he leaned back in his chair. "This is a video of a *truly* giant man. *Two*, presumably. Perhaps one of us should Google 'world's tallest man' and let's just see how implausible this is."

Tariq walked over to an ancient looking terminal at the back of the room, logged into his Al Jazeera account, executed a search.

After a few minutes, Tariq called back, reading the English aloud, paraphrased: "Robert Wadlow was 8 feet 11 inches tall when he died at the age of 22 ... he was abnormally tall due to hypertrophy of the pituitary gland ... come look at the picture."

Faruq and Ahmed approached and looked at a picture of Robert Wadlow standing next to and dwarfing his father. The photo was over 60 years old.

"If what we saw is true, we have seen a gentleman who is *two feet taller* than this fellow," Faruq said, "And I have to say that he looked like he was in proper health and not ... *abnormal* ... like this person." He felt a twinge of guilt at the word he had used in his assessment.

A minute passed with no sound but the gentle humming of the equipment in front of them. Faruq leaned over Tariq and took possession of the mouse, navigating back to the Google home page, pushing him aside and typing in the single word 'giants' and hitting enter. In less than 2 seconds, he was rewarded with a list of hyperlinks.

"I am thinking he does not play third base for New York," Faruq said as he scrolled down past the top choice. The third selection was the Wikipedia entry on 'Giant (mythology)', which he clicked. *"Here* we go," said Tariq, "The giants Fafner and Fasolt seize Freyja … it appears that you have accidentally stumbled upon a group of looters choosing to reenact the Ring of the Nibelungs inside the burning Baghdad Museum – during an air raid, no less!"

Although Ahmed's first impulse was to box Tariq's ears, he couldn't help but chuckle a little at the thought. He scanned the sections of the Wikipedia entry outlining giants that appeared in Greek mythology, Hindu mythology, the Bible.

There was a list of a tall skeletons that had been discovered around the world, but few appeared to be well-substantiated. "Useless," Ahmed said, changing his focus from the computer monitor to the larger monitor behind them displaying the frozen image they had recently captured.

He dropped into a chair and rotated it to face the others.

"First of all, let us dispense with this whole 'are we crazy?' business and discuss plain facts, yes?" he said. He stroked his beard and began, "What we are looking at is not *only* abnormal, but it is expected to *be* abnormal. We can only presume that the other burqa is disguising a similar giant, stooped over and covered. One only employs a disguise when one is attempting to guard something important from casual observers."

"Well, of *course*," said Faruq with a cough, clearing his throat. "I guess you mean to say that we definitely *saw* what we saw – so we can simply conclude, "These two so-called men are in fact … *giants* … and their existence is meant to be a secret. A secret that we now have videotape evidence of."

The three exchanged meaningful glances. Ahmed began replaying the drive back to the Al Jazeera Baghdad headquarters in his head, wondering if they truly had not been followed. Faruq was thinking along the same lines.

Tariq was imagining a large sum of money, having no clear idea how this pixelated gigantic person would actually translate into the swimming pool full of dinar, but having no problem simply skipping ahead to the dinar and the bikini-clad women with bottles of ambrosia and loose morals …

"So what *exactly* are we looking at?" Faruq asked, all three men returned to the screen, looking at the giant enter the black truck.

"We see two giants and perhaps five men with them who are looting the Baghdad Museum. *Successfully*, we should say. They appear to leave with two large sacks full of – who knows? – and a small metal case that one of the uniforms brought out. In the meantime, another group of men with guns comes onto the scene and attacks this contingent. *Unsuccessfully*, it seems to be."

"This second group of men may or may not have known anything about the looting, but the jeep is not a police or military vehicle, neither Iraqi nor American … but I cannot understand why they would stop and engage the giants-and-company unless they perhaps were there to loot the Museum as well, yes?" Ahmed offered.

"I have to imagine that they were looking for something specific," Tariq said, deciding to play along with the thought experiment while keeping half of his brain committed to fantasies of intimate oil application. "If you're interested in money alone, why not loot the bank behind which you two were ensconced? Why steal things that are publicly known to be held by the Museum and therefore hard to sell?"

Ahmed took a pause, enjoying how fast ideas were keening about his brain.

"I just don't understand how it is there are men out there who stand eleven feet tall and this is the *first time* I've ever … *we've* ever …" The other two nodded in assent, waiting for Ahmed to continue.

"Given the global news organizations and the Internet, and … let's be frank … a *goatload* of human eyes and ears on the planet … do you *understand* what I'm saying?" said Ahmed.

"You lost me at goatload, my friend," Faruq responded, experiencing a mock punch to the arm.

"Let me call Qatar and see if they've received the feed yet. We did watch it *once* without pausing while transmitting," said Tariq, standing up from the seat and walking to a phone across the room.

A low whistle became audible shortly after he stood up. The whistle increased progressively in pitch until it was replaced with the last explosion any of the men assembled in the control room would ever hear.

As the ceiling buckled downward, the picture tubes along one side of the wall concussed and spat tiny shards of dull glass fast enough to eviscerate Ahmed and Faruq where they sat, embedding themselves into Tariq's back as he felt his feet lift off of the floor.

A violent swirl of pressure and wind twisted his body in a corkscrew fashion as a fireball erupted across the descending shards of ceiling, setting Tariq's hair on fire. Mercifully, all three men were unconscious at this point. By the time they were buried in rubble and melted plastic wires and charred wood, they were all dead.

Chapter 8

David made his way down a slight incline in the foothills just south of Beth Shemesh. He carried with him a light spear and a sling, and six rocks with medium heft rested in a satchel lashed to his waist. There was no one else in sight, and for the fifth time he had just about convinced himself to turn around and go home before steeling himself by closing his eyes and thinking of Michal.

The intermittent bushes and fig trees offered some cover, but he really required more *distance* than cover. Peering at the ground ahead, he saw a few more remnants of wool smeared with blood, and continued along the path demarked by large paw prints. He crept to the end of a tree line and scanned the hills that lay before him, directly beneath the midafternoon sun. Twenty feet towards the hills, another piece of wool.

Should he have brought Raddam and Ozem with him? Should he have, in Yahweh's *name*, at least told them where he was going? It was not unlike him to disappear for a while with his sling and spear to go hunting or to practice with his weapons.

It had been some time since Abigail had made fun of him when he did so. Perhaps Abigail felt differently now that Eliab, Abinadab, and Shammah had all joined Saul's army, and their homestead had become that much emptier and quieter.

Eliab was twelve years his senior and fit his role as the eldest as naturally as a tunic on an Amelikite. Everything David knew about swordplay had been taught to him by Eliab, who had taught each and every one of his brothers how to fight properly.

They were descendants of Judah and knew from a young age that they were expected to keep the Commandments of Yahweh – and in return, the lands west of the Jordan River would be theirs in perpetuity. David had grown up fearing and loving the Lord.

He approached two neighboring hills, riddled with trees and brush, paused to listen. The wind rustled through the canopy of the forest and the birds in the forest were excessively chatty.

He padded his way to the edge of the forest and made his way over a hillock to a natural line dividing the two hills. He felt with some degree of certainty that he and his brother Nethanel had come this way before. A smear of blood on a rock was tellingly slight. He was nearly certain that the trail caused by a sheep losing its last few ounces of life was coming to an end. From this moment on he needed to rely on the providence of Yahweh. Pray for the slight wind to send his scent *away* from the path ahead.

This – what he was doing right here, right now – was *ludicrous*. He was going on faith that the lion that had claimed one of their sheep was alone in the wilds, having neither a family nor an entire pride to contribute food to. This faith relied on a single fact – that Abinadab and Shammah had taken him along two years earlier on a similar hunt, over similar terrain.

It was important for him to never be so far away from trees that he could not find himself high up in one the *instant* danger presented itself. Entering a forest made this fairly straightforward. Lions tended to be wary of human beings, understanding intuitively the lethal intelligence they possessed.

Lions would defend their territory and their cubs, but were willing to negotiate on precisely what constituted their territory when confronted with men holding spears and wielding slings.

David continued to walk north, doing his level best to remain silent. Remaining silent was something at which he was quite good. The youngest in his family, he had found himself the focus of the attention of his mother as a child, and negotiating the rivalries and bonds and eddies of familial antipathy became a specialty.

Through it all he felt closest to Eliab. As the oldest, Eliab had adopted the mantle of responsibility, stepping up naturally to be Father's second-in-command, helping to run their farmstead, raising hundreds of sheep and growing enough alfalfa and hay to feed them, as well as spelt and oats to be made into bread. There had been thin seasons, but most years had been free from want.

Thirty yards ahead of him he could make out a hollow curving into the hill on his left, and the hairs on the top of his head stood on end. Surely it was Yahweh issuing a warning of some kind, reaching into his natural instinct and ratcheting up his senses to drink in everything necessary to survive this encounter. And he *would* survive this encounter, he was sure. He had a destiny and there was *no* mistaking that, and he had known this since he had first dreamt it at the age of ten.

Shammah was the one who had instructed him about Yahweh, who had proscribed the Commandments that inspired the Laws of Moses, followed in spirit if not to the letter by all the faithful in Israel and in Judah.

Shammah had committed to memory the stories of Cain and Abel, of Abraham and his son Isaac, of Esau and Jacob. He had related the story of the Flood, when Yahweh saw fit to save Noah and his family but destroy the wicked humans – and to attempt to wipe out the Anakim, which were an abomination in the Lord's sight.

Not far north of Jerusalem could be found the worshippers of Baal, and according to his sister Zeruiah, these humans shared a *different* opinion concerning the Anakim, and on the charge of Yahweh.

She did not elaborate on what she had heard, but David had little interest in these stories ... with one exception. He had heard rumors of a Ceremony of Fire celebrated by the Anakim and other worshippers of Baal. He had to confess that anything with the name 'Ceremony of Fire' was worthy of contemplation.

In the end, he spotted the lion before the lion spotted him. It was a single lion. He did not care why at the moment. The lion lay nestled in a clearing encircled by evergreen trees and brown weathered rocks.

She was intensely occupied with her dinner, which must have helpfully distracted her from smelling David as he approached. She clearly had such large teeth and claws that she feared little of what she might encounter in this clearing.

And now he crept. The grass was tall and it was impossible to swim through it without marking some signs of passage, but Eliab had taught him well. Eliab had also taught Abinadab well – it had been Abinadab who had made the final passage years before, using stones to stun the lion in question and his spear to finish it off, just as David would do today, Yahweh willing.

His approach took him to a large boulder at the southernmost tip of the clearing in which the lion was gnawing on a leg with great satisfaction. He peered around the side of the boulder and locked eyes with the lion, who had begun monitoring his approach with some interest, but not enough to distract it from the feast between its forepaws.

David nearly lost control of his bladder. He was grateful not to, feeling this might detract from his legend – a legend he had crafted over many lazy summer days in his childhood when it was too hot to work.

Reaching into the satchel at his side, he selected a jagged rock and fit it into his sling. He stood up, and the lion twenty yards away growled lowly, gnawing with less enthusiasm, wondering if this animal was half as stupid as his bare-skin frame looked. The subharmonics emerging from her throat could easily have been mistaken for a chuckle.

David began to spin the sling, slowly at first, increasing in speed. Swish, swish, swish.

It was a sound he could close his eyes and interpret – good swish, steady swish, bad swish, and he made adjustments with every circle. By this time, the lion – *lioness* – had stood up and her low growl metamorphosed into a dull roar of annoyance. For this pathetic specimen, her dinner had been *interrupted*? She had the faculties to imagine how much saltier the air would taste with his red, crimson life sputtering out of his neck, ten seconds from this moment.

David released the stone. It sailed through the air and struck the lioness above her right eye, drawing free-flowing blood and causing her head to rear back in immense pain. She was stunned in surprise and cried out. David loaded the second rock, began padding closer into the clearing, began spinning his sling in a tight circle.

The lioness on instinct felt there was a best course of action to take – she turned around and began to run, smacking straight into a tree and rebounding, dazed.

David released the second stone and it struck her in the ribs, cracking one of them, making it painful when she roared in protest. He began to run towards the lioness, who found herself limping confusedly into the path of a boulder, unable to determine the best course of flight, eyes sticky with blood.

David brought down the spear into her side, thrusting hard to the left, causing an immediate and powerful response from the lioness, who whirled counterclockwise with such force the spear was ripped from David's hand and smacked against the boulder, splitting its handle in two.

David began backing up rapidly, fumbling in his satchel for another stone as he did so. With her one half-clear eye, the lioness trained on David, meaning to tear the throat out of this aggressor, bunching up her rear leg muscles in an effort to pounce, distracted by the throb and injury.

As the lioness leapt, David threw the stone with his bare hand, striking the open mouth of the lioness, cracking three of her teeth, one of them nearly knocked loose from her maw. The stunning, blinding new pain caused her arc to miss David's torso, but her front right paw tore into flesh before her weight carried her rolling in a ball into the center of the clearing.

She struggled to regain her footing. David ignored the warm fluid running down his left arm as he jumped to his feet and inserted his fourth stone into the sling, climbing on top of a boulder to do so. His protective measure was unnecessary. When he let loose the fourth stone and it struck the top of the skull of the lioness, she staggered left and right before collapsing in a heap, straining to breathe due to a punctured lung.

David approached the lioness from behind warily, the pain in his left arm reaching his mind through the effects of shock.

He watched her struggle with each breath, clawing forward to slide her body away from him, one inch at a time. Without conscious warning, he began to cry. Tears started to roll down his face as he stepped forward slightly, watching a suffering animal, knowing that it was suffering because of him.

By the time he came to the lioness and removed the half-spear still embedded in her side, thrusting it into her again, he was almost convulsing from sobbing. With the third thrust, the lioness stopped moving. David stopped moving.

He didn't return home with the body of the lioness for another two hours.

Chapter 9

The next morning, they continued along the river, heading northward towards its source. The events of the previous night seemed like a dream.

A large, uncovered, glowing man had come into their midst and had engaged them in strange talk, and then he had turned to look skyward. After a minute of silent communion with the sky, he had departed without a word, heading back north in the direction from which he had come.

There was little debate in the morning. Jophet and Siroc discussed the entity that had visited them the previous evening, trying to determine whether it was a threat to them. If it was, should they devise a means to attack it, if it returned? They had weapons that would likely cause some damage, but less to *it* then it could to *them*, surely, even though the entity was – to a fault – weaponless.

They had brought Mehujael into the conversation. What manner of beast had they encountered the night before? Was the encounter related to the appearance of the lion days before that?

These questions tended to cause Jophet headaches, were dismissed by Siroc as meaningless and distracting, but Mehujael seemed to thrive on such questions. As they spoke, a woman approached them and asked, "May I join your counsel?"

"You wish to join this counsel without your husband?" Jophet asked.

"My husband is fishing," she answered, and sat down when Jophet motioned to her with a nod of the head.

"I did not perceive this man as a threat," said Mehujael, "What I found disturbing was that it did not seem to be my … *mind* … telling me this man was no threat." He had used the word for skull in their tongue, and it struck him as apt, as had dozens of new words coming into said skull these past few days. "The knowledge entered my *mind* from somewhere else."

"If it had been a bear," said Siroc, "I would have been afraid as I plunged a spear into its body. But every thought I had to drive a spear into this man changed into a thought of putting my spear down on the ground next to me. My … mind … is not entirely *open* to me – as you might say, Mehujael – but I think we all experienced something unlike we've ever experienced before."

Siroc was not typically long in speech, and the others took this to mean an implicit allowance that talk might be more effective to deal with this new experience than a spear would be.

"I do not believe it was a man," the woman said plainly. "And I know how crazy this is going to sound, but I feel that this man is the exact same creature we encountered in the shape of a lion." And as soon as she said the words, the others knew them to be true.

"Which may explain why the man appeared to be naked but I do not recall having any kind of – let us say, *womanly reaction* – to this state, as opposed to the feelings I had the first time I saw my husband naked."

Mehujael turned a deep shade of crimson and Siroc burst out with a gut laugh that lasted a full ten seconds before sputtering into a minor coughing fit. Jophet said with a slight grin, "I believe that I as well had a quite different reaction to seeing this being last night compared to the first time *I* saw your husband naked."

"And while we talk about instinct, I have to add a curious note," she said, picking at the frayed edge of an animal skin dangling from a skinned knee. "He seemed to be telling us last night that we were not permitted to travel north, as if this were his *territory*, but that *isn't* what he was saying, and somehow I understood what he was saying beyond the words he was using."

"And what was he saying?" Jophet asked.

"I don't believe that you need me to tell you, although I will be happy to. My husband felt the same way I did, and I'm curious how you three felt. What did he actually *say*?" she asked in return.

Jophet stroked his bearded chin and replied, "For some reason, we may not be permitted to travel further … but it is not *his* decision. I think he left to get that decision."

"You are telling me that this gigantic man who appears like magic, like fire and rain and wind is magic, who can be a lion or can be *us*, but *moreso* – this man needs to ask permission from *someone else*," Siroc outlined.

Jophet nodded. Mehujael nodded. And Siroc said, "And if the answer is no?"

"I believe the answer to that is obvious," the woman said, "We would turn around and go south, would we not?"

"Even though we've been heading north because … it feels – *right* – to be heading north …" Jophet said, looking at the others in turn and seeing no one contradict him.

An hour later, camp broken and possessions stowed, the tribe of men and women headed north.

They made camp that evening near the shore, as they had before. This time, they did not see a distant glow before they *perceived* a distant glow, and they knew in their chests they were about to be visited again.

It came as a shock when they were joined by *two* large glowing men, one slightly shorter than the other, but each more than twice as tall as Jophet. And Jophet, having given the matter and the counsel a lot of thought over the course of the day, simply motioned for the two men to seat themselves in the middle of the group, by the side of the central fire in the clearing. The guests did so before they spoke.

"What are you called?" asked the taller of the two, the one who had come the previous evening. Jophet was about to answer, but then he stood up and called over the husband of the woman who had joined them for counsel that morning.

The husband approached the inner circle and remained standing, chin nonetheless raised to look into their faces in spite of their being seated on the ground.

"We are … *men* and *women* … we call ourselves *humans*," he answered somewhat meekly.

They nodded to each other, and the shorter one asked, "May we?"

During the following morning's counsel, it was again remarked upon how strange comprehension entered their minds from outside of themselves, a thing that was simultaneously as comforting as the embrace of a mother and as terrifying as thunder. At the time, they all understood, and the man next to Jophet simply said, "Yes."

To which the two giant men bowed their heads and began a communion similar to others they had engaged in before, but for all intents and purposes was the first instance in history.

We call ourselves *humans*, the man had said, and the giant beings perceived in the man's mind a distinct picture of humans, and this was different from the picture he had in his mind of a monkey – *his* word then, *monkey* – and in his mind of a lion – his word then, *lion*.

Many more pictures appeared in some common shared abstract space that Jophet experienced peripherally, due to his proximity … *jaguar* … *snake* … *bird* … *worm* …

No one spoke for five minutes, and there was no fear. Siroc no longer felt any kind of threat. Not literal. No sense of threat he was attempting to manufacture just out of the sense that he *ought* to.

The giant men brought their heads up simultaneously, and a spell was broken between them and the man next to Jophet.

"And what are *we* called?" the taller one asked. And from some conduit the word came to him, as new words frequently did, although seemingly not from the same source as usual.

"You are *Nephilim*," he said, and the word felt right to everyone.

"Thank you, Adam," the taller of the Nephilim said.

Part 2

Chapter 10

Javan and Lemuel sat in a dimly-lit basement in the Rasheed district of Baghdad. Although they sat stooped on a bed, neither would have been able to sleep comfortably in that bed, and indeed, it had yet to be determined where the two *would* sleep that night.

If worse came to worst, one of them would be lucky enough to fold his body in some semi-fetal position and attempt to sleep on the bed while the other would stretch out on some old pillows on the ground and try to cover his body with two or three judiciously-placed blankets. At this point, it was all but inevitable, and a coin flip would determine who got the bed.

The pillows would be brought down by their hosts later that evening. The floor was empty, save two large black sacks and an iron chest. The two Anakim fixed their eyes on the iron chest. "I really think it's *your* duty to open the chest," Javan said with assurance.

"It is absolutely my duty to open the chest," Lemuel said, "But is there any sort of *hurry?*"

It was a careless question to which he knew the answer – the answer was *yes* – and it was kindness Javan was showing him not to force the issue, although Javan had always creatively interpreted his duties, and when it came to Lemuel, Javan was willing to stretch this interpretation to the limit.

They both turned at the screechy sound of a poorly-constructed door being inched open, and a parallelogram of light became visible twenty feet from where they sat, up a flight of stairs that had taken them a long time to negotiate, and which had barely supported their weight when they had ambled down them, one at a time.

The silhouette of Ajaf appeared in the light. Hearing no protest, he walked down the steps and crossed the nearly empty floor to stand in front of the iron chest. Ajaf had tears in his eyes.

"Jamal is dead," he said simply. Lemuel effected a look of empathy he had been trained to employ with humans when they were neither laughing nor yelling.

Javan remained impassive, but anyone who had known him as long as Lemuel had – over seventy years – would have known that the news had been devastating to him. Javan had first met Jamal when Jamal was six years old.

"Thank you, Ajaf," Javan said. "Is there any other news?"

Ajaf snuffled and recovered, clearing his throat for a good five seconds. "The American invasion is going to make it difficult to get you to Jordan," he said, "But after that, we have good friends who will secure your passage into Lebanon and back home thereafter …"

Javan nodded, thoughtfully.

"Oh …" Ajaf continued, holding out a folded piece of paper.

Javan took the piece of paper – it was a fax that contained a scrawl of characters Ajaf had recognized, but could not read. It was not Arabic but did have a slight Middle Eastern feel to it, if Ajaf went by gut instinct alone. Javan saw the characters when opening it partially, saying gingerly, "This is probably for my eyes only, Lemuel." Lemuel nodded feebly in reply.

It was awkward for Javan to read the fax in a manner that would keep it hidden from Lemuel. The height of the basement ceiling was not large enough for him to stand erect, and he was barely able to slide to an angle on the bed so that Lemuel could not see what was written.

Even this precaution was nearly pointless – Lemuel would *not* try to read the fax; he would be content to hear whatever news it contained that Javan *deemed* he should hear.

After reading the contents of the fax, Javan asked Ajaf for pen and paper to formulate a response. When Ajaf took the paper from him, he knew it would be faxed to Damascus, rendered into white noise in transit thanks to a chip that had not come from the human manufacturers of the machine – and then transmitted thereafter in a more traditional fashion. Ideally it would not be more than a few hours until he had a response to his response.

By this point, Lemuel had raised his head. Ajaf had left. Javan looked at him expectantly.

Lemuel reached over and grabbed the iron chest with his large hands. He dragged it to his feet and opened the lid, the lock upon which had already been crudely destroyed. The chest contained a series of papers and journals and books. Lemuel removed the entire contents so he could return them to the chest in reverse order and thereby make an inventory.

"Technically speaking," Javan said, "I shouldn't really be here for this part."

Lemuel gave a dismissive snort. He looked at Javan with a mock suspicious gaze and turned back to his inventory.

"I'm just saying," Javan said with a laugh. "Perhaps we are taking too much liberty with the roles we've adopted, that we've made vows to uphold. We deserve a bit of a scolding from Roland."

"Roland is not here," Lemuel said as he replaced the papers into the chest, pretending for the moment to be the one between them *less* concerned with protocol. "Mishik was remarkably prescient in her estimation of the contents of this chest. It turns out that Hussein wasn't *bluffing*, though we were pretty sure of that …"

Lemuel read the titles of scholarly papers: "*The Piltdown Man Hoax as Deliberate Obfuscation*" … "*Missing Skeletal Remains from the 1800's*" – papers that had never seen publication.

He came across a journal from an archaeologist who had excavated a site near Hebron. Came across the personal papers written by a scientist who had worked with Robert Fulton in the late eighteenth century – claiming to have been part of the New Amsterdam Project to effect optimal energy generation from geothermal sources – accompanied by elaborate, well-drafted diagrams.

"You almost have to feel sorry for the vicious tyrant," Javan said with an ironic sneer, "Do you think in the final days before the invasion he thought to call American President Bush and offer him evidence of the world's best-kept secret in exchange for a postponement of hostilities?"

"He did not actually *make* this offer?" Lemuel asked with some alarm, but Javan just laughed.

"To my knowledge … to *our* knowledge, this offer was never made," Javan said, slapping Lemuel on the back in a friendly manner.

Lemuel returned his comrade's look of assurance with one of acquiescence. It had only been twenty years since their paths had diverged, when each of them had had to decide what they would do for the next seven decades or so. Each of them had chosen as anticipated by their mentors, by their *bakhati*. It was rare for these decisions to be otherwise for the Anakim.

"We can at least return having completed a successful extraction here," Lemuel said, "According to your intelligence, we have recovered each skeleton and *all* of the documents Hussein was known to possess. We can return to Carmel knowing that our calculated risk was a just and justified one." He said this with a tone that begged confirmation, validation, a second.

Javan paused just a shade too long for Lemuel to remain hopeful.

After that moment had passed and Javan and Lemuel both knew that that moment had passed, Javan turned away from Lemuel and stared straight ahead at the wall across the room. Twenty seconds later, Lemuel exhaled the word: "What?"

Javan stood up – not fully – but he couldn't stay sitting any longer. He duck-walked a few steps away from the bed, whirled and sat cross-legged on the other side of the iron chest.

He fixed his eyes on Lemuel's eyes and assessed the conflict between obligation and duty and the need for a successful mission, and there was more than enough justification for full disclosure. His only reservation was knowing that Lemuel would be wary of full disclosure.

"Omar was all but sure he'd seen men observing our confrontation with the Republican Guard," Javan said, resting his chin on his fists, "Satellite imagery confirmed this. Tactical got an identification on the white van that left its position two blocks south of the Museum – and traced its route to the Baghdad Headquarters of Al Jazeera."

"This is a news organization, yes?" Lemuel asked warily, already knowing the answer and not really desiring to hear the confirmation, "Please go on …"

"I know you might not quite believe this … well, I guess you *will*, given our history … but I'm not sure how the following happened by extraordinary coincidence …" he began, looking for the right words, "Evidently, an American missile strayed off target and happened to strike this headquarters building."

Lemuel inhaled sharply and felt embarrassed by it. Then he reveled in the embarrassment. After all, that's why he chose the path he did for his Years of Vocation.

"Not a coincidence," he said quickly and flatly.

"Surely not a coincidence," Javan echoed, looking at Lemuel with some sympathy, but realizing that the divergences of their life paths only allowed for so much sympathy. Furthermore, that difference delineated who they were as beings, and continued friendship relied on an elasticity of sympathies.

"But …" Javan continued, opting again to pull back the curtain into his thinking farther to the side than Lemuel might prefer, though would not protest, "*Disproportional.*"

And almost just a little too *timely*, if a coincidence, Javan refrained from saying aloud – and his gut instinct was telling him they would soon learn that it was *not*.

Their conversation was interrupted by the slamming of a door upstairs from where they were sitting. Light appeared again at the top of the stairs, and Ajaf ran down them awkwardly, holding out another folded fax to Javan.

"This one just came across the wire marked URGENT," he said between breaths.

"Thank you," Javan said again to Ajaf. Ajaf was just shy of seventeen – already six foot three inches tall and only recently having left the mountain for the second time to return to his family.

For a brief moment Javan thought about his *own* Walk through the Fire, and his memory brought sharp focus to the present, so he quickly opened and read the fax that had been placed in his hands.

As Ajaf closed the door behind him, Javan looked up to Lemuel. He decided to ignore protocol and simply handed the paper to Lemuel. Lemuel read it. "Five dead. More to come. They transmitted the video," he said.

"They transmitted the video," Javan echoed.

Chapter 11

In the center of Sokoh was the war room. Three Philistine generals were gathered at a table poring over a crude map inked onto animal skin, using stones of different colors to represent the encampments of Saul and the regiments of the Philistine army. Their barking and prattle served to reinforce the shadows that lay thick underneath a pair of eyes watching the generals make plans.

"This is *necessary*, of course," said Kenaz, who stood with a look of disdain, standing a full seven feet tall, wearing horsehide that had been treated with particular oils to toughen it, a short sword hanging at his side. He turned to his right and looked up at his deflated companion.

"I *suppose* so," said Goliath, folding his broad arms across his chest. He was dressed similarly, though the hides Goliath wore required fifty percent more material, and the sword he bore was sturdier and more ornate in design.

"It's just … this used to be our *library*," he said with no hidden sadness and exasperation. "The wall behind those men and their runners used to be *full* of skins and clay tablets and the flat, more ephemeral material that the Egyptians use. Of course, it's likely that the average septacentenarian might contain more information than what was held here in this small building …"

Without a word to the generals, they quit the building via the exit to the east, finding themselves in a courtyard with a huge brass sundial at the center. Stone benches lined the outside of the square and they made their way to the nearest. Goliath sat down comfortably and Kenaz stood across from him, now able to speak face to face.

"I really don't understand this," Kenaz said, "As long as man is putting up sword against man, why do you to consider yourself their stewards?" This alone was a provocative question to ask a giant, so he had no incentive not to throw out another: "And if so, why are you *quitting* the city?"

Goliath regarded Kenaz warmly, sure that they had started this conversation ten years earlier, when Kenaz had finished his last year under the mountain, undergoing the Rite of Moloch.

"We are stewards of the *Earth*," Goliath said, and the sentence seemed familiar to Kenaz.

"The Earth of Yahweh or the Earth of Baal?" Kenaz asked, finding the words familiar as well, part of a half-remembered liturgy. If he had begun the dialogue in the hopes of making a point, or of learning something new, then embarking on a well-trodden path would not yield results.

Goliath answered by rote, "There is only *one* Earth."

With that, they became silent, and Kenaz positioned himself on the bench next to Goliath.

They said nothing as people walked back and forth between the war room, through the courtyard, to the streets leading past what used to be the commerce district of Sokoh. They were both struck at how *empty* the city was, how much less lively. There remained no women, no children, no young Anakim.

Suddenly, a man ran breathlessly into the courtyard and headed towards the war room but stopped short, having easily spotted Goliath seated next to Kenaz across the way. He padded his way quickly towards them, and they patiently waited for him to recover and speak.

"Goliath, you have a visitor," the messenger said, and Goliath detected from his accent that he was likely someone they had placed in the Israelite camp to keep watch on the movements of Saul, which immediately ruled out the visitor he had most longed to see. That, of course, would have been impossible. "Please, follow me."

Goliath stood up and once again found himself four feet above Kenaz and nearly twice as tall as this young man. "What is your name?" he asked.

"It's Simon," he said meekly, somewhat cowed walking next to the imposing figure Goliath presented. "Your visitor waits for you at the Temple of Life." Goliath slowed his gait.

"The Temple of Life?" he asked, "But …"

"He is *Anakim*, sir," Simon said, "He said his name was Talmai."

Goliath abruptly *stopped.* Goliath almost asked Simon if he were *sure*, but the question was silly, and it was time to move on, and he felt some distress at the potential meaning of this visit.

He looked ahead at Simon and Kenaz, both of whom stared back somewhat confused by Goliath's reaction, prompting him to shake the cobwebs from his head and simply make his way to the Temple with no further interruption.

As they approached the Temple, Kenaz turned to Simon and said, "We're not really allowed in there."

"Really?" Simon said in confusion, "Because Talmai brought me in there ten minutes ago and told me to go get Goliath."

"Okay, yes, technically we can be *permitted* to enter … but … look, Goliath … Simon and I will return to the war room and wait for you there, okay?" Kenaz said with a wave. "Simon can tell me whether or not he was able to relay to Jonathon the latest 'intelligence' on the Anakim."

"Not *directly*, of course," Simon said with wide, honest eyes that made Goliath smile. Kenaz pulled on the shoulder of Simon's robe, causing him to pivot from conveying an important message to making himself completely scarce. They turned to walk back up the footpath north while Goliath squared his shoulders and headed towards the entrance of the Temple of Life.

They had not passed a soul on their walk there. They had not *expected* to. Goliath did not expect to see another Anakim for at least a week, and all of that depended on what Saul did next. He certainly did not expect to see a tetracentenarian risk his life by coming to Sokoh on the eve of the next battle with the Israelites!

He entered the Temple, finding all curtains and draperies removed, walls empty of extraneous material as perhaps all of Sokoh now was. Just the essentials. As he entered the central chamber, he saw an altar upon which a single goblet was set, and in the middle, a fire pit devoid of anything flammable.

A dead Temple, no longer holy. Talmai stood next to the altar, a face bearing notes of levity and dignity alike.

"Goliath," he said warmly, "I cannot tell you how pleased I am to see you. You cannot imagine how heavy my heart is to see Sokoh a *skeleton*, a river with no water, fire with no flame, like intimates divided by deception ..."

Goliath nodded and reached out his arms, crossed at the wrists, clasping Talmai's hands in his. "And more killing to come of course," Goliath said softly, "More killing and more killing and more *killing*."

Talmai regarded Goliath sadly but had no words to contradict him.

"More killing," he echoed.

"And our best guess is that this continues to be the *will of Yahweh*, as far as Saul is concerned?" Goliath asked, feeling somewhat impetuous at one-hundred twenty.

Talmai did not nod and did not answer, but chose rather to let Goliath find his own response – to let his instincts find an approximation of the answer to an approximation of the question Goliath had actually posed.

"Why are you *here*?" Goliath asked suddenly, abruptly, annoyed that he had forgotten the biggest question that had been on his mind. "Is there something wrong *with* – " and his heart went cold. *Dead* cold. And he found it impossible to draw a breath, to complete the question.

"No, *no*!" Talmai said, "Baal and Yahweh willing, *no* ... I have not been there for some time, so I cannot give you any news, unfortunately. You haven't had word ... ?"

"For two weeks, Talmai," Goliath said swiftly, "I just worried that your appearance here was meant to prepare me for something truly awful."

"No," Talmai said yet again, "It's not like that. I'm not here with *that* kind of news. I'm here because we're nearing the culmination of a *century* of planning, and the oldest of Anakim are endlessly debating the merits of the plan. I continue to bridge the gap between the oldest of our number and the youngest of our number."

Talmai laughed at that, and laughed again, laughter turning into a coughing fit, one that Goliath tried to relieve with judicious slaps to his back. Though somewhat advanced in age, he was in no danger from the harsh treatment.

"For all intents and purposes, I believe that Saul considers this the last stand of the Anakim," Goliath said, removing his sword from his scabbard and waving it around in a haphazard, ineffective swirl. "Which is the *point*, of course."

Talmai removed a candle and swished it around the air in a similar manner. He continued laughing and broke into nothing less than a guffaw, clearing his bronchial passages of no shortage of fluid, and Goliath could not help but join him in a soul-cleansing laugh that emanated from their guts, leaving them weaker for it at the end of a minute.

Following that, a sigh or two. Following *that*, Goliath put his arm around Talmai and said, "In all seriousness, Talmai – is there any possibility that Saul and his people truly feel that they are in any meaningful communion with Yahweh?"

Talmai regarded Goliath soberly. He considered the question thoughtfully, trying to read from Goliath's face that the question contained any notion of literal interpretation.

"It's hard to say," Talmai said with a tone of naked honesty, "Have any of us *communed* with Yahweh or Baal in the memory of our kind? *Truly*? Do we understand our charge correctly or are we just deluded? And even if we understand our charge, are we living up to it in the slightest fashion?"

Goliath broke from embrace with Talmai and fixed an eye on him that was correctly interpreted as a desire for a fuller answer.

"I *do* think that we understand our charge and I *do* believe we are doing our best to execute that charge. And mind you, I have taken three times as many steps traversing the path of *my* life, Goliath," Talmai said, "I simply choose to believe those old stories hold meaning, as if the truth of this world can be a *choice*."

"You've no doubt listened to Leph tell those stories many, many times," Goliath said, and again felt a pang for home and family and those closest to his heart, and had no idea how far away any of them or any sense of returning to the life he most desired actually was.

Chapter 12

The two Nephilim had been with the humans for a week. The tribe had only broken camp twice during that time, preferring frequently to stay in place, to relaxing in clearings along the great river, enjoying the abundance of fruit found in the trees of the forest.

Two of the humans were walking with the taller of the Nephilim in the forest. "Your husband gave a name to my companion," the Nephilim said, now in a perfectly modulated and articulated voice.

"*Michael*," said Mehujael, "But *you* do not wish to be named. As an *individual*."

"I am not sure it is … *permitted*," the Nephilim replied, "It is not a matter of my … *wishing* …" And although the pause had been before the word 'wishing', both humans sensed that he had hesitated in using the word '*my*'.

"Tell us again why you first came to us," Mehujael requested.

This was something the Nephilim had discussed only in the most abstract terms, but with every day that went by, they more open, more able, to engage in speech, speaking with increasing specificity.

"We are meant to watch over the world," he said, "To … *keep* it. It is our responsibility."

"And who gave you this responsibility?" Mehujael asked.

The Nephilim halted, finding that they had entered a grove of trees where he was having to speak through a throng of leaves to make himself understood. As a group, they made themselves comfortable and breathed in crisp, clean air in quiet contemplation.

"You have to understand that these … *words* … you use …"

"*Language* is what Adam has decided to call the sum of our words and the rules we use to combine them," Mehujael said, recognizing the sophistication of the concept and of the sentence he had just constructed in their … *language* … and that it was more sophisticated by some degrees than his thinking had been a mere four weeks earlier.

"Yes, *language*," the Nephilim said, "It is insufficient for me to communicate with you, but it seems to be the only mechanism by which I *can*. It is not the same manner in which I communicate with my creators."

The two humans looked at each other with curiosity. Could it be possible for this being to have been *created*?

"Who created you?" the woman asked, reaching over to touch the Nephilim's knee. It was an impetuous gesture, but in the daylight, his inner glow was nearly absent, and it confirmed for her that his knee had the same texture as her own, as Adam's.

"I feel as though I would know deep in my being if I were not supposed to answer your questions. After all, we grow closer and closer to the *Trees* ..." he said after some deliberation. "I will do my best to tell you what I remember."

Mehujael and Eve looked at each other with some excitement. The presence of the Nephilim had served as a large frond in fanning the flames of their curiosity. Others had been more excited to walk with Michael, who was teaching them which plants were safe and which ones were to be avoided, and talking about what plants required in order to be healthy, and how that differed from the needs of Jophet's tribe.

"I have been alive for a long, long time. Of this I am *sure*. And yet, my memories only go back so far – memories of swimming and of running and of flight ... As you know, I have not always had this appearance. It has been Baal and Yahweh, I believe, that have determined my appearance over time," the Nephilim said, then refraining from speech for a long pause.

In the wake of the sentence they could not parse, the two humans patiently waited, and eventually, the Nephilim shook his head back and forth slowly.

"No, I don't think *that* is true either. I'm not sure they created me, but I know that they are *older* than me, more *powerful* than me ... and I owe my *life* to them. I would not continue to exist without their *assent*. As if I'm ... an *appendage* ..."

And Mehujael and Eve suddenly knew the word 'appendage', and in so doing, solidified their understanding of the concept of metaphor.

No one spoke for a while. "I know I am meant to *protect* you," the Nephilim said, looking to Eve and Mehujael in turn, "Though I'm beginning to feel like the responsibility of protection has become more difficult with you ... *humans* ... given your natures. I can tell you definitively that the world has never before witnessed the likes of you. I don't know where your kind began or how long it took before you made your way here to Eden ..."

Eden, both Mehujael and Eve heard. A name given by this Nephilim, rather than Adam.

"As we have already told you," said Mehujael, "We're not sure of these things ourselves. But our resources in the south had become insufficient, and Jophet has led us on this journey ever since ..."

Eve looked up at the Nephilim, seated across the clearing from them. When he had first appeared, his eyes and his hair had been abstract and indistinct, but increasingly they had depth and features.

Were he a man, the features would have made him attractive to most women, but as she'd noted before, there radiated from him an aura that dampened any sense of physical attraction.

Whether this dampening was intentional, or simply instinctually felt – whatever the source of or the nature of this dampening, it did not eliminate *every* kind of attraction.

"I think that perhaps it is time for me to return to Yahweh and Baal and get more direction. I cannot feel them strongly enough from here to enter full communion," he said with some regret. He stood up, and with no further words of farewell, walked into the forest and was soon out of sight.

Chapter 13

"Let *me* do the talking," First Lieutenant William Majors said calmly, taking a long pull on an unfiltered Camel cigarette and flicking it casually out the passenger's side window. He turned to the tall, lanky Iraqi teenager behind the wheel and smiled reassuringly at the seventeen-year-old.

Ajaf nodded fitfully, unable to disguise the butterflies in his stomach. He turned back to look through the windshield at the caravan of trucks coming to a halt on the highway to Al Basrah.

Wind was blowing tiny cyclones of sand along either side of the road, and they spotted a delegation of soldiers emerging from the second truck, an M36 that had surely seen better days.

Ajaf swallowed hard and elected to leave his hands on top of the steering wheel, clearly visible. He turned to the older man he had met twelve hours earlier and found enough courage to say, "May I ask you a personal question, Lieutenant Majors?" The lieutenant smiled more broadly.

"*Bill*, please," he said, having enjoyed Ajaf's desire to practice his English as they headed south. "We may have just met, but given our shared heritage … well … I need not elaborate …"

Ajaf nodded thoughtfully. Having never met an *American* with his shared heritage, he appreciated the casualness with which this had been expressed.

A young corporal was leading a contingent of five men toward the spacious black truck that Ajaf had powered down two minutes earlier, after Ajaf had seen the flashing red light on top of the lead truck in the convoy.

"You are a military man," Ajaf said with some nervousness, though his recent experiences had emboldened him beyond his years. "And you have sworn an oath of loyalty to the United States of America." Bill turned from the approach of the men and met Ajaf's eyes again.

"To the *Constitution* of the United States of America," Bill said with a hint of mirth amidst solemnity.

"To the *Constitution*," Ajaf repeated.

"Are you asking me how I feel about our current activities in light of that oath?" Bill asked. Ajaf simply nodded, having misgauged the amount of time it would take for the men to reach them. They both silently thought of the two burqa-clad Anakim who were making themselves comfortable in the back of the truck, no doubt wondering why the truck had come to a halt hours ahead of their destination.

Bill noted the swiftness of the men too, so he responded succinctly, "You would be surprised, young man, how easy it is to reconcile every oath I've taken in my life, both aboveground and underground ..." Smiled only slightly, then nodded towards the window next to Ajaf.

The teenaged driver turned and quickly moved to roll down the window just as the group of men arrived alongside the truck. The two privates at the rear of the unit held M4A1 carbines loosely at their sides.

"Corporal," said the lieutenant with ease, holding out a folded paper to the man at the window with his left hand, saluted briskly with his right.

The corporal returned the salute, lowered his Ray-Bans, made eye contact with the lieutenant and with Ajaf, nodding slightly. "Lieutenant," he said hoarsely, unfolding and reading the document he was handed. Looked up with widened eyes. Bill Majors simply nodded.

Corporal Mark Davidson walked to the side of the truck and sized it up, letting his eyes run down its length, eyes looking low, high, fixing themselves at the biohazard symbol and requisite, unnecessary warnings in English and in Arabic below.

"Lieutenant, do we have Saddam dead to *rights*?" he asked in a thick Southern accent. Bill took the folded orders back from the corporal and merely grinned.

"Not at liberty, corporal," he said simply, and not five minutes later, Ajaf turned over the ignition and resumed the journey toward Kuwait.

First Lieutenant William Majors knew that the next part of their trip would take much longer and be more prone to discovery by an overly cautious ally without some support.

Having conferred with his superior officer in Pennsylvania, arrangements had been made to pick up an escort. Twenty miles south of the place they had been stopped, their black truck was outfitted with red flashing lights and joined by a string of Army personnel carriers and jeeps heading south to Safwan.

They were all stopped at a final checkpoint, and once again Majors' papers brought them into Abdali, Kuwait, without a second glance from the man who held them in his hand for less than three seconds.

●

An hour later they pulled onto the tarmac of the Ali al Salem Airport. As the back doors of the truck swung open, the two burqaed Anakim found themselves face-to-face with a fat, balding, sunglasses-bedecked, robe-clad, cigar-chomping, walking Middle Eastern cliché.

Leaning into the cliché, Raoul opened his arms widely with a bellowing "Friends!!!!"

Lemuel and Javan had been able to stretch their legs and arms out in the truck, so now they had the displeasure of resuming a stooped hunch designed to make them look like fat, Sharia-observant women.

As they carefully stepped down, Raoul's companions scrambled into the back of the truck and returned with a newly-sealed iron box and well-stitched-up black bags. Bill Majors was shaking Ajaf's hand, clapping him on the back as Ajaf opened the driver's side door. Ajaf took a last look at the two Anakim in disguise, in his side mirror, chest swelling with pride as he turned over the ignition.

"Those are to go to Mount Carmel," Javan said from under the burqa-mound closer to Raoul, who turned from watching Ajaf drive away.

"And my, what a deep *voice* you have, my dearie," Raoul said, rubbing his hands on his stomach as he chortled. If it were possible, the shoulders hidden under the burqa appeared to sink even lower.

"Honestly, do you two have *no* sense of humor? You will like me more when you see the accommodations on my private jet!" This, Raoul punctuated with Groucho-Marx-rising eyebrows as he twiddled his cigar in front of his mouth.

After long hours in the modestly air-conditioned truck, they were indeed pleasantly surprised by the accommodations.

The modified Boeing 747-400ER was taller than they were by a comfortable margin. What ordinarily would have held two floors of passengers and a floor of baggage and cargo had been modified to include a section meant to accommodate four traveling Anakim in an analogous form of first class.

Javan and Lemuel took seats in the second of two rows, each designed to hold one Anakim and one human on the left, comfortably, and the reverse in mirror image on the right. Between two hallways on either side of the back of the cabin, a tall door stood adjacent to a lighted sign inviting all comers to the rest room, as indicated by icons showing two stick figures side by side, one twice the height of the other.

"Please feel free to refresh yourselves after your arduous trip here," Raoul said, pocketing his sunglasses. Behind him, two attendants had begun securing the cabin.

"May I take your burqa?" asked a sweet-voiced, honey-haired attendant wearing an immaculate gray and black uniform, standing nearly seven feet tall.

Lemuel's eyebrows went up slightly, hearing English for the first time in some time. Although First Lieutenant Bill Majors had conversed more than adequately in Arabic, he also appeared relieved to hear English as well.

Lemuel readily returned to the language he had immersed himself when he had been forty-two years old, one year before he underwent a program of immersion in Italian.

"Yes, please. And if it could be laundered before we arrive in Qatar, that would be most appreciated," Lemuel said, dusting off bits of rubble and concrete specks from the black garb and handing it to the tall woman. Javan tossed his over to

Lemuel and entered the restroom, not having to stoop at all to enter the twelve-foot-high doorway.

"What can I get you to drink, Raoul?" the attendant asked her new employer, having just been hired by this man she knew little about.

It was sufficient to know that not many private citizens could have engaged the services of her peers, or of her. She was determined to keep her ears open, as she could not deny being intrigued. "And for *you*, Lemuel?"

"Ice water would suit me fine, miss," Raoul said.

"I would very much enjoy a coffee, miss ..." Lemuel said.

"Fatima," she said with a smile, "You will have your coffee, and we shall be in the air in approximately fifteen minutes."

"Yahweh's balls!" Javan cried upon exiting the lavatory, "Lem, they have a *working bidet* in there. Constructed for an *Anakim*, I should say ... with, well ... requisite *force* ..."

"Can you imagine the one they asked to hold still for measurements so they could *make* that? And what did they tell the company who constructs bidets?" Lemuel asked with amusement, feeling weary beyond measure.

Unable to contain his curiosity on other things Anakim-sized in rooms designed for comfort and convenience – which he understood to be rare in most places the Anakim spent time in, outside of their cities – Lemuel dashed into the lavatory before his coffee arrived.

Shortly after Lemuel had returned with an unfettered smile, everyone got situated for liftoff, which was smooth and uneventful as the Boeing jet lifted into the sunset sky.

Minutes passed and Raoul said, "We will be in Qatar in less than an hour, and I know you two must talk. I will excuse myself, and this cabin shortly after will become sound- and signal-proof. You will still have working phones should you need them. Anything else?"

Lemuel said, "Do you have access to the Internet on this jet?"

"Of *course*," Raoul said, pulling out a drawer from a table that sat in the center of the room between the two rows of seats. Raoul flipped up the screen on a laptop and turned the computer on.

"Do you happen to know if the nearest Internet-to-Undernet router is in Kuwait?" Lemuel asked, seeing incomprehension, and then he rolled his eyes at his own statement and said, "But of course we are not on land, and this will hit a satellite first … I'm sure the connection will be fast enough …"

"It may be that my English is failing me," Raoul said as he exited the room. "Please use the intercom button to call for Fatima or for me. The pilot will announce when the landing is imminent."

Bill Majors looked curiously at Lemuel, "You surely are not just intending to check your e-mail, I presume …"

"No," Lemuel answered, "There are some bulletin boards of interest I need to monitor. The transmission of the video of … *me* … has been sitting in Qatar now for over 24 hours. I might be able to determine within a short span of time whether the video has … well, *migrated* at all."

Javan sat pensively, head turned to the other two. "Strictly speaking, we're supposed to keep our plans on dealing with this situation separate," he said to Lemuel, who had been thinking along similar lines, "But we're not really being given a lot of guidance here."

"The Council of Allegheny is deliberating a course of action," Bill said. "This is a bad time for this to be happening. Our best intelligence had all but eliminated the possibility that Saddam had any kinds of weapons of mass destruction, let alone any progress towards a nuclear program, but now that the U.S. have struck a nest of wasps with a baseball bat, this is our best chance to confirm our best intelligence."

"But Lemuel here was engaged to learn if the rumors of what was in the lowest level of the Baghdad Museum had any sort of *basis* …" Javan said, "And rightly so, I should point out – the right decision *was* made, I have to say. Still, here we are and it's not clear what network resources we'll be able to avail ourselves of when we arrive …"

"I would really rather we not bombard their Doha Headquarters with missiles and kill more people unnecessarily," Lemuel said softly with a sigh, "I really don't do well with this calculus of killing people to save people."

"Five people versus five billion, Lemuel?" Javan asked, and Bill nodded solemnly. Still, Lemuel couldn't help feeling a bit sick to his stomach.

Chapter 14

Jonathon was seated at a table with Eliab, Abner, and Shammah, eating a meal of lamb and olives and dates. The entire mood throughout the dinner tent was subdued. In twelve hours, they would advance on Sokoh and begin the siege, uncertain whether the humans and Anakim inside would launch an attack immediately or simply dig in.

"I really don't understand," Shammah was saying, wiping his mouth on a burlap napkin, "Why did they abandon every city near Jerusalem save Sokoh? Do they really expect we will suffer them to remain there?"

Abner grunted assent and Jonathon looked a bit perplexed. "According to our intelligence, the Anakim maintain today what they maintained in the time of Joshua. It is the will of Baal and the will of Yahweh that they must safeguard this world," Jonathon said.

"They hope to achieve harmony among *all* things that live in this world, but they cannot even achieve harmony between its various peoples and tribes."

"To say nothing of the fact that Yahweh has *forsaken* them!" Eliab said, punctuating the statement by pounding on the table with his empty goblet.

"It is *blasphemy* for them to continue to maintain that they somehow speak for Yahweh, or understand what Yahweh wants. Yahweh has given the Israelites a *mandate*, has given us permission to retake these lands.

"By Yahweh, we are *doing* so … our only setbacks occur when the people become faithless … begin to entreat Baal to provide better crops and so forth, as if Yahweh's punishments were somehow *unjust* …"

Abinadab got up from a neighboring table and came over to sit between his two brothers and Saul's son, across from the commander of Saul's army. "Are you so *sure* that Yahweh has forsaken the Anakim?" he asked somewhat meekly.

"My only experience with the Anakim is from the time Father and I went to their city in search of charity for our starving family," he continued, "We met one of their number who was called Bog, and he spoke to Jesse all afternoon about his crops and his animals, and told him what he could do to survive the drought and – I believe there was something he called 'crop exhaustion'."

Shammah turned to Abinadab and looked at him as if his brother had just lifted his robe, dropped his undergarment, and began knocking their goblets over with his privates.

"*Brother*," he said with undisguised disdain, "Samuel has made it clear that the Anakim are *despised* by Yahweh, and that the Flood had meant to wipe *them* out every bit as much as the wicked humans Noah was surrounded by."

"And yet the Anakim somehow survived that Flood," Abinadab replied in a mock conspiratorial tone, "Did they cling to the underside of Noah's ark? Either Yahweh had told Noah to invite *their* number onto the ark or they were able to survive in spite of Yahweh being *against* them. And doesn't Samuel insist that *none* of us would survive, if Yahweh be against?"

Abner had finished his meal and stood up, excusing himself from the table.

"I believe that it is far easier to put my faith in Saul. He can tell me Yahweh's will, and I merely follow *Saul's* will. Saul, a man in front of me who I can touch and argue with," Abner said in parting, "You might do better not trying to determine directly the will of Yahweh. It is arrogance to assume that Yahweh would directly provide guidance to every single individual …"

"Do we really trust *Samuel* as a prophet?" Abinadab asked, "Just because he has memorized to a comma every piece of the Law of Moses?"

Jonathon's face turned red slightly, though he was unsure why, but then thought it might be because of all the references to unclean women found in that Law, and thinking about those references had always embarrassed him.

"Samuel has the sanction and favor of Saul," Eliab said.

"And Saul the sanction and favor of Yahweh, according to Samuel," Shammah said, lowering his voice slightly, as their heated conversation had attracted the attention of at least twenty other young men in the dinner tent, all of whom were a bit gloomy and in need of distraction.

"Which I must confess is the kind of thing that always seems a bit too convenient," he continued, "But I tend to agree with Samuel on the Anakim. They are bigger and more powerful than us and they live many, *many* years longer than we live. If it were not so difficult for them to bear children, they would have long ago run over the land, brought every human tied up, screaming, to the high places, and tossed each one of us into the fire."

"Does that explain why they would leave all of Israel and Judah except one city?" Jonathon asked, coming back to the first thing Shammah had said at the start of the conversation. "Perhaps they can hold it for a while, but not *indefinitely* ... and they know we are coming ... *why* are they staying?"

Around the table, each man thought they had more to say, but all were silent as they finished their dinner and goblets of water.

Eliab was the first to spot their youngest brother clearing plates at the other side of the tent. "David! Lionslayer! Come over here when you are done with that table!"

David looked a bit sheepish at being singled out among the evening's servants to the soldiers, but shortly after disappearing with an armload of plates and goblets, he returned and came to sit with his brothers.

"*Lionslayer?*" Jonathon asked quizzically. His eyes darted between Shammah's and David's, and David grinned with a modest façade that was hard to mask with bravado. David was unaccustomed to holding his cards closely to his chest.

"There was a lion who had killed *two* of our sheep and was dragging them back ... well, to her family, I presume," David said, suddenly envisioning four hungry lion cubs crying for a mother that would never come back again ... and it took a hearty clout on the back from Shammah to dispel the horrible picture from his mind.

Eliab stood up abruptly from the table, causing his empty goblet to spin in a circle, teeter towards the edge, fall to the ground. "And fierce David followed the trail of blood and wool with nothing but his spear and sling!" Eliab shouted, beginning to stomp about the dinner tent.

"And the mighty she-lion sat with her kill in the forest until … *roar!*" Shammah spat, up now in the tent and facing Eliab, fingers raised in claw-grasps, rolling his head as if tossing a mane that the imaginary lioness had not in fact possessed.

"So David went like *this!*" Eliab yelled, grasping Shammah's left wrist with his, spinning him around to the right and reaching around Shammah's right side from behind, using his right leg to attempt to bring down Shammah's right leg.

Shammah's wrist was too tightly bound to squirm away, but he brought his right leg back, knelt down, tossing Eliab over his shoulders and onto a quickly-cleared table adjacent to where the others sat.

Shammah intermittently looked at Jonathon, but Jonathon was regarding David as if he required the close visual image to complete whatever mental image Jonathon currently had in mind.

Shammah shook his head mildly.

"Suffice to say," David said to Jonathon, "I killed the lioness and brought her back home. Evidently, Mother says the lioness will provide meat for a few meals for the farmstead." Jonathon smiled at the thought of seeing a baked lioness with an apple placed in her mouth.

"That was incredibly brave," Jonathon said, smiling broadly at David. David adopted a chaste look, unable to stop from saying, "You wouldn't mind relaying that story to Michal when you see her next, would you?"

Eliab and Shammah stopped in mid-embrace, Eliab's hand grasping Shammah's hair and firmly pulling the head back, Shammah's arm locked under Eliab's knee. "The *devil* you say?" Shammah said while releasing Eliab at the same time he was released.

Eliab guffawed. "Brother!" he exhaled, "You are as see-through as the *River Jordan* …"

David glowed bright red and began gathering goblets from the table. Eliab grabbed him from behind and lifted him a foot above the ground. "You really have some cheek making sheep eyes at the king's daughter!" Eliab said in a mocking voice. David, however, was fairly immune to his older brothers.

"Father won't let me have glory in Sokoh, so I will take glory where I can get it," David said, "And I won't lie and say I am *not* utterly captivated by the king's daughter, and I could not care *less* who knows it."

"Clearly not," Abinadab said with a laugh.

And Shammah did not stop looking at Jonathon, who had not stopped looking at David for the past three minutes.

Chapter 15

Michael had remained with the humans in Eden during the weeks that the other Nephilim had left them to commune with Yahweh and Baal.

Under his direction, a huge contingent of humans fashioned and nurtured a garden within the Garden, and reinforced their own knowledge of growing things they could eat. He continued to show them things that were poisonous and things that surprisingly were *not* poisonous. Annika had less than two months before she would give birth, and one day Jophet had decided that they had traveled far enough along the river.

The pull they had felt leading them ever northward was absent. Eve tried to engage Adam in conversation about this strange change in everyone, but it was the sort of conversation he would not readily engage in. Mehujael *did* engage in this conversation, though was still preoccupied with the novelty of thinking about thinking.

One summer evening the humans and Michael were once again gathered around a series of campfires at the side of the river, enjoying reenactments of their early travels presented by Mirab. Slightly altering the routine, Mirab was silent while providing exaggerated movements while Zillah related the story.

Zillah spoke with a commanding voice, and the story she told was not perfectly literal. Some of the humans struggled to understand the meaning, and all of them were captivated when Mirab and Zillah finished the reenactment – and then began a new story.

In this new story, two young hunters were pursuing a tiger that had been threatening their camp. It became clear without any explicit words that Mirab represented the stronger hunter of the two, and Zillah was trying to disguise her fear, not wanting to look like a coward in front of her friend.

Adam found himself perplexed, feeling that this was probably Siroc and Bart … no, Siroc and Vedic … no … who *were* these two men?

The hunters came upon the tiger while hiding in thick brush on the edge of a forest, and Mirab outlined the plan of attack to Zillah with a complicated series of hand gestures. While Mirab turned to where the tiger was in the minds' eyes of everyone, Zillah turned to the crowd and attempted to repeat the series of gestures, but to her (his?) dismay, could not seem to recall them correctly.

It was clear to the audience that Zillah did not understand the plan, and many young hunters felt some alarm, waiting for Zillah to ask for clarification … and she *wasn't!* And they understood that Zillah was afraid to ask out of embarrassment at not understanding, and they felt similar embarrassment.

"Who *is* that?" Nephem asked loudly, and her neighbors shushed her. Michael sat nearby, occupying significantly more room than the humans about his feet.

Eve was enraptured and could not stop smiling. This was purely … *magical* … and unlike anything she had ever experienced in her life. And her alarm grew at the same time there was no cause for alarm, and she enjoyed the dissonance of alarm and not-alarm as Mirab and Zillah ran to attack the tiger.

Some of the young boys and girls stood up on their feet, unable to bear the tension when Zillah not only positioned herself in the wrong place, but also tripped and fell on the way to it. Mirab made it clear by her actions that suddenly the tiger was upon her, and she fought against it with a club in her right hand and a rock in her left, but the tiger was now clawing at her torso, at her face. Zillah stood paralyzed with fear for what seemed to everyone present an unbearable amount of time.

Finally, Zillah summoned courage, picked up a stick and a rock and ran to where Mirab remained under attack. She joined Mirab in the fighting, but Mirab did not look strong any more. Zillah made a final circular motion with the stick and then appeared to watch as the tiger ran away. She threw the rock at where the tiger had appeared to be running to, and the audience understood that the tiger had been successfully chased away.

It was equally clear that Mirab was not able to lift her head off the ground because she was deeply wounded … and soon clear that she was mortally wounded. They watched silently as Zillah threw her head to Mirab's chest and looked distraught. Without warning, Zillah felt her mind depart from Zillah, and she felt raw truth in lying on top of her dearest friend, her fellow hunter whom she had failed.

Without intending to, she began to cry. A stream of tears made its way down her cheeks, and she lifted her face to the sky and wailed. Seconds later twelve of the women, two of the men, and nearly all of the children had tears running from their eyes. Tears of sorrow for a friend who had died, and again Nephem shouted, "Who … *is* … that? I don't remember one of us dying at the hand of a tiger!"

Mirab suddenly opened her eyes and sat up. Zillah stood up and Mirab joined her. They turned to face everyone else in their tribe, smiling. There was an explosion of relief as all tension drained out of their audience.

"This is the story of Tamil and Radu facing Tiger," Mirab explained. Or failed to explain. There was no Tamil, nor was there a Radu among them, nor had there ever been.

While the crowd murmured amongst themselves at the strangeness of this story that had never happened, Eve suddenly stood up pointing north and shouting, "Look!"

The others followed her finger and traced a path into the darkness that ended in a very familiar glow. Michael stood up, and an almost imperceptible smile turned the corners of his mouth. They were being joined by more of his kind.

Five of them, specifically, and all were still slightly indistinct, as the original Nephilim had been when first appearing as giant replicas of the humans. Unlike that original appearance, they already wore robes that covered them as the humans did, as Michael had taken to doing shortly after his time spent with the humans.

With six giant Nephilim in their midst, the humans remained unafraid.

It soon became apparent that the Nephilim were having some kind of discussion, though their lips did not move and there was no sound.

Siroc stood closest, waiting to be addressed, somewhat curious as to why so many of them had come. Eve was not alone in wondering where the original Nephilim was – she found herself avidly awaiting a reunion with the being with whom she had passed many afternoons.

She walked to the edge of the clearing and gazed north into darkness lit up partially by a quarter moon. No one else was approaching, and she felt distinct disappointment.

The Nephilim only spoke briefly to the humans that night, letting Adam come and give names to them all. The humans soon began to feel fatigued and made their way under skins, huddled together, sleeping soundly in the temperate night

The next day it was nearly two hours after everyone woke up and had begun preparing breakfast that Adam noticed that Eve was no longer in their camp.

Chapter 16

"I could get used to this," Javan said with slight disingenuity, sinking into the folds of an amorphous red velour chair, admiring the solidity that bore his three-hundred fifty pounds with enough give to provide comfort, but not enough to make extrication awkward.

Lemuel was scanning the room as he circled it, reaching up to trace his fingers along the smooth ceiling, still a good two feet above the top of his head. He had not set foot in such a house in seven decades, had not really spent appreciable time outside of the mountains in ages, and he chose to relish the novelty.

"Is this common in the human world?" Lemuel asked, and Javan exhaled in a half-chortle, shrugged.

"I rather doubt it," Javan answered speculatively, zeroing in on the bronze sculpture Lemuel stood before, ceasing to pace. "We obviously have a number of wealthy benefactors in the world ..."

"*Homikim*, though, is it not so?" Lemuel said at a low volume, unsure where in the house Raoul was, a house he understood Raoul to own, though that simple fact had never been explicitly stated by Javan. For a brief moment, he found himself seeing the world through Javan's eyes, and with them, scanned about the room for any indication of audio or video monitoring of the basement.

Javan looked at his friend of a half-century with a look of mild appraisal. "Raoul is *not* Homikim," he said with careful deliberation, assessing Lemuel's facial response. "To be sure, there are giants in his ancestry, but not recent enough that he spent time with us in his youth ..."

"But ...?" was all Lemuel could articulate as his attention returned tangentially to the sculpture near him, which he reached out to touch, impetuously and almost unconsciously.

"But *indeed*," Javan said, holding close to his vest the fact that he had only learned some of this in his most recent conversation with Halakan, his primary bakhatu, who lived in Alpenheim.

The door fifteen feet behind Lemuel opened with a creak, and before turning, he wondered whether the timing of Raoul's return had anything to do with the turn in conversation.

"Forged by Velus," Raoul stated, gesturing with his right palm raised. A young man they had not previously encountered took a position to the right of the open door as Raoul strode toward Lemuel. "Anak the Younger debating Socrates in Athens."

Javan looked appraisingly at the holstered Jericho 941, raising his chin in slight acknowledgement to the man before he rose to his feet and swiftly crossed the room towards Raoul, if only to gauge the man's reaction.

"Velus," he said after coming to a halt near Lemuel, folding his arms, looking acutely at the sculpture for the first time.

"The Anakim sculptor who created this in Xinjiang shortly after the Magna Carta was signed," Raoul said softly, sighing as he beamed at the piece with pride. "I have one of his final creations in my home in Dubai … *The System of the World* … leaning far more into abstraction than your kind tends to lean …"

Lemuel's brow furrowed, transparently searching his memories for mention of Velus, or of Anak the Younger, while Javan kept his features passive, his take on Raoul quickly reconfiguring itself. This only led to the conclusion that his need to reconfigure was Raoul's intent, and he would now have to replay all conversations with this man from the past 48 hours through a new lens.

"How did art from under the mountain find its way to Qatar?" Javan asked, making every effort to keep an accusatory, doubtful tone away from the question.

"A septacentenarian from Alpenheim sold these pieces at a Gray Market auction to raise money for victims of the Shoah," Raoul said, "But these are the sole details I could ever get my father to tell me before he passed."

Javan took this in and filed it away in a location he would revisit after the current emergency had been dealt with. He simply nodded thoughtfully, tying this thread into a terminal knot.

"I understand you will have operational needs at this juncture, and want to assure you that everything you need is at your disposal, and that you will be given total privacy," Raoul said, gesturing toward workstations on desks, hosting sturdy chairs meant to accommodate larger frames. "Internet, Undernet, secure fax to local Homikim households. I am monitoring my own sources, and will bring any news to Lieutenant Majors or me."

Bowing slightly, Raoul turned on his heels and exited the way he had come, the caricature he had presented at their first meeting absent. The young man who had entered with Raoul pulled the door shut as he left on the heels of his employer.

Each of the giants waited for the other to break the silence.

"I guess I am nominally in charge and I have to say that first and foremost, until we hear otherwise directly from our leadership, you and I should feel permitted to share information more freely than we might ordinarily," Javan said.

Lemuel nodded. No argument from him. Such an argument would more likely come from one who shared Javan's vocation, the vocation whose goal was to secure the Anakim and to maintain the secret of the existence of the Anakim from the majority of humanity.

"I didn't have time earlier to check everything I needed to on the flight," Lemuel said as he sat himself down in front of a terminal whose keyboard was roughly twenty percent bigger than a human-sized keyboard.

"I can say with reasonable certainty that there has not yet been any kind of public posting of the video that was shot in Baghdad, which is a *relief*. But I have not exhausted a set of smaller, private bulletin boards that are sometimes used for these kinds of postings …"

"I have only limited intelligence on Doha. There are several hundred Homikim families in the city, and our support in Carmel is currently contacting a subset of them to assist us tonight," Javan said. His brow furrowed.

"To be frank, I am extremely concerned at how exposed we have made ourselves. This week has been … *unorthodox*. It's folly that we are involving ourselves physically in this kind of intrigue.

"There were compelling arguments for you to go in person to the Museum, and I was glad to accompany you to lead the security detail. But our continued, extended walkabout borders on *insanity*."

"I think we passed a Burger King on the drive to this house," Lemuel said with understated mischief, "We could save ourselves some trouble and just reveal ourselves there …"

Javan exhaled the ounce of levity he would allow himself.

"The last fax we received on the jet was from Halakan. He deemed our direct involvement at the Al Jazeera Headquarters a *necessity*," he said, "Respectfully, I disagree."

Javan was on his own terminal, accessing utilitarian interfaces into databases to access the vast repository of information stored in the Undernet data banks around the globe.

"Ah! Here. Mohammed Al-Qamrun, cameraman and editor at Al Jazeera, employed there since 1998. His family has been Homikim going back four generations. Through the Fire in 1990 after spending his second year living in Fantale … how did I find this before Halakan's people?"

"My expertise with all things digital and analog and electronic will not be needed, then … and you will not be needed to protect me," Lemuel said, large fingers dancing over the keys, "We could stay here and order pizza."

Lemuel suddenly thought of Fatima – honey-haired, hazel-eyed, bringing him coffee on the jet, looking up at him with unbridled admiration. He felt a sharp pang of absent comfort, of longing to return to the safety of his tedium under the mountain two thousand kilometers west of Doha.

"Mohammed is not answering his telephone," Javan said, terminating with one click a low-volume rhythmic buzzing emanating from an application on his monitor.

Absentmindedly he opened another Vulcan browser and commenced a combined Undernet/Internet search that yielded a news article that jolted him alert.

Lemuel caught the change in Javan's body language in his peripheral vision. He had been reading posts to a bulletin board maintained in California concerning sightings of Bigfoot, but was seeing nothing concerning, and turned to ask Javan why he looked so pale.

Javan continued to scan a day-old article on a fire that had destroyed the home of one Mohammad Al-Qamrun, survived only by his six-year-old daughter.

"This … cannot be a coincidence," he said flatly as he met Lemuel's gaze.

He inhaled deeply, bowed his head in thought, returned Lemuel's fixed gaze, and said, "I don't want to get into details, but the errant missile that hit the Al Jazeera offices in Baghdad was a bit of a last resort. There was a reporter working in those offices named Ameen who was Homikim, and we wanted *him* to find out who had been sent to the Museum to gather a report …"

He trailed off, clearly distracted by other threads working their way through his mind. Lemuel waited patiently. Javan cast that thread aside. Jumped to the chase.

"You and I are being directed to *physically* go to the Al Jazeera Headquarters tonight," Javan said, "And I cannot *begin* to tell you how bad an idea that is …"

Lemuel was still trying to parse the sentence about Baghdad, and could not fully make heads or tails of what Javan was saying. Javan stood up abruptly and resumed pacing about the basement room, trying to sort events out in his mind. Again, Lemuel waited patiently.

"I'll try to summarize what appears to be happening," Javan said soberly. "We have an escalating crisis – given the existence of video evidence that Anakim walk the world."

Not just *any* Anakim, Lemuel thought as his stomach pitched.

"It's not the first time this has happened, and we have gotten good at destroying such evidence before it gets widely distributed. For the most part, this is easy to do given our … *reach* … into human affairs."

Lemuel nodded, knowing that his friend was far more aware of the logistics on how Homikim help was solicited and guided. Javan stopped pacing and planted himself in front of the sculpture of Socrates and Anak.

"It may just be a coincidence, but it feels as if our path is … *intentionally* … being made more difficult," Javan said. "The fact that we will have to don burqas and engage Homikim with lock picks to proceed in this mission, risking much, is a far-from-ideal path that I'm beginning to feel we are being … *placed* … upon."

Lemuel and Javan regarded each other, and Lemuel felt he understood what Javan was driving at, and felt he may be on to something with his deliberations. It added to his general trepidations, and once more he found himself just wanting to be back in Carmel, safely hidden, deeply hidden, his worries at an absolute minimum.

At this point the door to the basement was opened and Raoul appeared at the top of the stairs, accompanied by several of the aforementioned Homikim.

Javan had hoped for more time to piece everything together, but a small part of him welcomed the additional challenge, almost hoping his paranoid musings had some basis in fact.

He posited that maybe there was a neck out there he might someday wrap his hands around, squeezing the life out of an antagonist that may or may not, at that very moment, have some serious devilment in mind for the world and for Javan.

Chapter 17

The sun rose over the eastern wall of Sokoh, faintly glinting off scores of Philistine helms.

Goliath had likewise armed himself, pacing fitfully along the southernmost corridor of the city, inspecting the impressive phalanx of helmed archers standing atop a wooden platform positioned four feet below the top of the southern wall.

The generals remained in the war room a quarter mile north of the archers' position, and runners would relay information back and forth between the generals and the commanders that stood near Goliath, periodically meeting his eyes and smiling. Goliath did not smile back.

"I estimate that there are at least two hundred Israelites making their way towards us, moving in loose formation. They are taking up a position roughly three hundred yards from our main entrance," a man called from the platform.

Several minutes passed before he continued, "They're sending a messenger."

"By all means let's receive him," said Barik, the commander of his garrison of fifty.

One of the older archers, Sep, turned and called over his shoulder, "You want us to receive him or you want me to *receive* him, captain?" He drew back his bow, and the archers in his company, some as young as thirteen, chuckled.

Barik ignored this. "Luther, take your men and open the small gate for this messenger. Escort him to the generals," he said, removing his helm and scratching the top of his head underneath.

"Goliath – I want you to be there when this messenger comes in the door. We need to reinforce the intelligence they have on Sokoh … and if you would, please accompany the messenger to the generals. I wouldn't mind hearing a synopsis of the message."

Goliath was grateful to have the opportunity to leave the front and nodded curtly. When the messenger entered the city of Sokoh through a narrow gate meant for humans only, he emerged into a wide space and encountered a man twice his height, a sword at his side that could cleave said messenger in two.

Goliath folded his arms across his chest, feeling somewhat ridiculous, distracted. The messenger took twenty seconds to compose himself, and he chided himself internally for it. Still, this was the first Anakim he had seen with his own eyes, and his reaction was not unusual.

"I come with a message from Saul, King of Israel," the messenger said, "Please, take me to your leaders."

Beginning to warm to the idea of the required theater, Goliath placed his hand on the hilt of the sword at his side, drawing it four inches out and then replacing it, absentmindedly, several times, before finally speaking.

"Come with me," he said, intonations one to two octaves deeper than normal.

They walked down the wide streets of Sokoh, entering the courtyard that led to the former library.

Goliath gestured to the messenger, who entered the War Room ahead of Goliath, Luther, and four men accompanying Luther.

Inside they found three Philistine generals, seven aides to the generals, several commanders accompanied by a few foot soldiers who were in the process of having their mission detailed. All heads turned as the men and Anakim entered.

"Sirs, this man bears a message from Saul, King of the Israelites," Goliath said, "He appears to have brought several hundred Israelites with him, bearing swords, spears, and other items best described as *unfriendly*."

The youngest of the generals smiled slightly, and knowing that the older two generals had no sense of humor made his smile broaden.

"Give us the message," erupted from his mouth quickly in an effort to expel breath from his body before it emerged as a laugh.

"King Saul wishes for you to know that all these lands are Israel and Judah, that they belong to the *Israelites*, in the name of Yahweh," the messenger said with a lump in his throat, "It is King Saul's request that you leave these lands."

"Did we accidentally build a city on *your* lands?" Goliath asked with folded arms.

"Goliath! Enough!" the oldest general barked, meeting Goliath's eyes with an utter absence of fear, and in that single crystal moment Goliath understood how spectacularly the Anakim were going to lose this battle in an effort to win the war, and he felt conflicted.

He marveled at how much more easily the Nephilim would have overseen the life in the Garden back when their forebears were still swinging through trees on any branches that would support them.

"I have a message for Saul in return," the oldest general said. "Tell him that the nation of Philistine and the Anakim recognize Sokoh to be neither part of Israel, nor part of Judah. The hospitality once extended to the Israelites is hereby revoked. Once you have departed Sokoh, we will not allow any Israelites within sight of our city walls, under pain of death. Can you relay this message to Saul?"

"I can," the messenger stated – calmly, he thought to himself with pride – and turned to leave the building. Luther and his men left with the messenger, escorting him back to the same entrance into Sokoh.

The generals as one regarded Goliath somewhat warily. They relied on the men under them to do their bidding without question, and it seemed clear to them why the Anakim had never properly formed their own military to take control of the known world. They had not met many Anakim who took the discipline and responsibility of military campaigns seriously.

Goliath read their eyes, felt keenly aware of what all of the men in that room were likely thinking. He sensed that they were eager to send him out into the field as their champion in two days' time, knowing that dead or victorious, they would soon be rid of him.

Shortly after noon there had been a quick charge towards the westmost section of the southern wall. The intelligence of the Israelites had led them to believe that this point would not be heavily guarded, and this was good intelligence.

A small group of runners brought a ladder with them while loosely protected by a separate group of men holding a tent of fabric over the assembly that effectively hid their intent as they progressed quickly towards the wall. Several heavily armed men also lay hidden under the makeshift tarp, and Shammah thought that this was a brilliant plan.

Only a single arrow found itself embedded into an Israelite, puncturing his neck artery mortally, forcing Shammah to take his position holding the tarp for the rest of the trip to the wall.

The terrain surrounding Sokoh was flat, giving no additional natural protection for the city. The walls were meant to be decorative and it had not entered the minds of the original architects some four hundred years earlier how easily one would be able to climb the wall with a simple ladder. There was little about the campaign of Saul they would have imagined at that time.

As the first Israelite reached the top of the wall, he was accompanied by a second with a bow and arrow. The fortifications hastily made in the past two weeks by the Anakim and Philistines did not extend this far down the wall. The platform that allowed their archers to counteract a central frontal assault could do little to impede this plan.

Just as a gang of fleet-footed Philistines reached the westernmost point of the corridor next to the wall, an arrow lodged itself into the chest of the fastest runner.

The other Philistines produced wooden shields and dove headlong at the six Israelites who had made their way into the streets while the Israelites nearest the wall assembled an apparatus of ropes that would allow them to retreat, provided they could secure this small street corner.

The melee at this corner of Sokoh continued for some time, with Israelites making their way to the wall by a path that left them only somewhat vulnerable to arrows launched by the Philistines that remained on the platform nearer the center of the southern wall of the city.

From the corner where the Israelites had planted themselves there were only two streets from which the Philistines could approach, and both sides settled into positions waiting for the others to make moves.

Those that did make a move found themselves taking out an enemy or two before succumbing to the blows of his comrades. In the meantime, Israelites had dipped some of their arrowheads in an oil that were set alight and burned as they sailed through the air, landing on a few nearby roofs, giving the Philistines another problem with which to deal.

The generals in the war room debated whether Saul was determined to make all of his moves on day one of the conflict, forcing them to commit soldiers to guard the corner of the city while a frontal assault was in the works. They held Goliath with them, trying to determine when and where he should be placed for maximal psychological effect, berating the Anakim for not providing them with a larger retinue of their number.

Goliath took their verbal abuse sedately, almost serenely. It only made it clearer to him that his people's plans for Canaan had been sagely decided, and he wondered if perhaps their broader mission concerning their shorter cousins was simply not worth the trouble.

The sun was an hour before setting when it became clear that the Israelites did not intend to press. The Philistine soldiers were amazed at their fortune. Half of their company had quit the city two days earlier and had marched three hours north to rejoin their main force. It had not been a secret to the infantry and street-level commanders that they had no intention of keeping Sokoh. It was now certain that Saul did not know this, or the battle might have been finished in a single day.

Rumors and gossip focused on the unshared plan for quitting this city with their bodies intact. They wondered at what deal had been struck between the Philistine generals and the Anakim. At the very least, it was clear that the generals had no intention of making the city's capture easy for the Israelites.

An easy victory in Sokoh might embolden the Israelites and give the Philistines no end to problems on the northern and eastern borders of Judah.

This intention underpinned the decision to send out a large party in the middle of the night to cut off one of the sources of food for the Israelites. And, at the same time, to secure some hostages that might prolong the drama of the struggle that was about to unfold.

Just before sunset the Israelites retreated from the corner of the city they had secured, climbing up knotted ropes with archers covering their retreat, removing ropes and ladder and sending out a few more flaming arrows before they departed from Sokoh and rejoined their camp.

When Shammah reported to Saul that evening, he told Saul that by his reckoning, they had killed seventeen Philistines and had lost ten of their own. Saul smiled at the numbers. The campaign was just beginning and he had demonstrated to the Philistines that they would not be able to predict what he would do next.

Saul had not yet heard news from Jesse, who was on his way to the camp of the Israelites. An hour later, Jesse would tell him how their homestead had been attacked, his son Raddai killed defending his sisters from the Philistines. The flock of sheep had been scattered and two of his sons taken prisoner.

At the same time Jesse related this news to Saul, the Philistine generals and Goliath sat in the war room regarding the two hostages being brought before them, bloodied from the physical conflict that had left them disheartened and subdued.

They were both clearly in a lot of pain as they were forced into the building with their hands tied fast behind their backs. They were greeted by the sight of an eleven-foot-tall armed behemoth who stepped up to them and asked to the men behind them, "Who are these men and why have you brought them here? They are not dressed as soldiers …"

One of the generals walked up to Goliath and reached up to his forearm to get his attention. "The Israelites get much of their food from the farms west of here, south and west of Bethlehem," he said. "One of these farms is owned by one of Saul's oldest friends."

The two bruised, beaten men looked up at the mention of Saul's name, not understanding any of the other words. Goliath felt uneasy. The general

continued, "That friend is named Jesse and these are his two youngest children."
Goliath felt more uneasy.

"What are your names?" Goliath asked in a Hebrew dialect the two men recognized easily. They were a bit surprised that the Anakim would know their tongue, and it prompted the younger of the two to speak.

"This is my brother Ozem," he said with some difficulty, given the condition of his jaw, "And I am David."

Chapter 18

What Eve was doing was clearly ridiculous, and yet here she was, continuing to *do* it. Continuing to make her way along the riverbank, heading northward, ignoring the gut instinct that was pushing her to go back. And ultimately, that is *why* she did not turn around after ten minutes. Because it was *not* her gut instinct. Not truly.

In *truth*, her gut instinct was aligned with her mind, and they were set on heading north. What compelled her to stay with her tribe, what had compelled her *tribe* to stay where they were after a year of living nomadically, was clearly something *else*. Mehujael had found the sensation curious and enjoyed thinking on it. In contrast, Eve kindled a growing anger.

The fact that the compulsion to stay was not an absolute mandate, as evidenced by her continued ability to *fight* the compulsion, tempered her anger somewhat. But it did not *dispel* the anger, and she wondered how many others felt the same way.

She had engaged Adam several times on the subject, but he seemed not to truly understand what she was talking about. He spent a lot of time with their two boys, both old enough to enjoy long afternoons of fishing with their father, their father attempting to name all varieties of fish and plants now, feeling it was his avocation, somehow.

And there she stopped.

Visions of Cain and Abel crystal in her mind's eye, and although they required less and less of her as time went by, there was a sudden piquant stab of feeling irresponsible, selfish. She turned back to look southward and felt her resolve waning. But did this feeling of being selfish come from *within* or was it being driven *into* her?

She sighed. The answer to that was obvious, and she turned back and continued to head north.

It was not right to let her family and tribe worry about her, so at worst she could be gone the day, but staying through the night would not be acceptable. And honestly, would they worry about her excessively?

Somehow, they had had no problems with wild animals in recent times, and it was understood that in some way that was due to Michael's presence. And this feeling of safety imparted by Michael's presence had oddly *not* quit her, three hours now hence from the tribe …

Michael. She reflected on the name while she made her way over a series of fallen logs.

She could force herself to string syllables together if asked to give name to some thing or some *one*, but the result would not have felt right, either to her nor to others' ears. Whatever it was that gave *Adam* the ability … perhaps simply the self-confidence and lack of desire to self-edit or overthink … *that* was what it had taken for Eve to freely and joyfully take Adam for her husband, and to father her children.

Many men in the tribe were strong and had captivating eyes, and several would even endure her incessant questioning – questioning which had predated these recent encounters with Michael's people. Yet Adam attracted her the more – and Mehujael simply had not seemed, *did* not seem, interested in physical forms of recreation in which most were interested, to include *Eve*.

She could hardly be faulted for feeling attracted to this nameless Nephilim, could she? It was not in fact nameless but *nameful*, she thought, a blank template containing pieces of Mehujael, pieces of Adam, pieces of Siroc … reflected pieces of Eve *herself*, she would argue.

Minutes later, her breath departed from her.

She had been forced by thick bushes and knots of tree-throngs to walk farther from the river, until at one point she could not see it from her path. Before becoming anxious about this, she had come to the end of a tree line and had entered the largest clearing she had seen for nearly seven months, when they had first entered this forest far to the south and west from their current location.

With a painful catch, her breath entered violently, and unbidden, a tear thrust itself from her right eye and trailed down her cheek and left her face, falling on a frond at her feet.

One hundred yards to her right, she could see the river emerge into the edge of a small canyon that created the appearance of an immense clearing. A waterfall fed the water from the river into a pristine lake at the bottom of the canyon, maybe thirty feet lower from the precipice upon which she stood.

The lake below was ringed with trees of all kinds: broad leaves, sharp-tipped leaves, evergreens … forming a canopy that shaded half of the lake from the sun. This canopy was dominated by a single, ancient, crooked, beautiful, *beautiful* tree … *Tree* … a tree that filled her with such awe she lost all strength in her legs and descended to her knees.

This weakness only increased as she scanned the rest of the basin and saw a similarly humungous gnarled tree emerging from the side of the hill on the other side of the clearing, with smoke emerging from a hole at the top of that rocky hill. Tears flowed freely down her cheeks.

This companion tree inspired nothing short of utter reverence, an emotion she had only felt in an infant state when first the glowing lion had stepped into their midst, and now she was crying *harder*, as if she could no longer take in more of the canyon.

"You are not permitted to be here," came a voice that startled her into utter panic, and she stood up and whirled around and found herself face-to-waist with the being whom she had sought … and her brain was finding it impossible to assign meaning to the words that had come out of nowhere, unexpectedly, and she began backing away from the Nephilim unconscious of doing so.

Her left foot twisted abruptly as she placed it on an unstable outcropping and her leg tumbled out from underneath her. "Eve!" he cried, leaning over quickly and grasping her wrist, wrenching her off of the ground and unceremoniously crushing her against his chest, his left arm closing the embrace to keep her from tumbling back down, dangling five feet off of the ground.

She yelped from the sharp pain, first to her left ankle and then to her left wrist, and then she was aware of her wet hot cheek against the chest of the Nephilim and she felt a warm vibration overtake her body, and she could not form a coherent thought for nearly five minutes.

For his part, the Nephilim had not felt human skin so hot and so close against his *approximation* of skin, and there was a mental swaying he had never encountered that seemed to fold in several weeks of knowing this woman in *eyes* and in exchanged *words* that continued to surprise … and he felt, perhaps, a surfeit of coherent thoughts, with the net result that he was unable to sort through the queue to convert any of these thoughts into words that might emerge from his approximation of mouth.

Eve had moved slightly away from him, held by his gigantic cradling arm, looking up into his face, seeing more human emotion in the lines and folds than she had yet seen on the face of a Nephilim.

"What is this *place*?" she asked quietly, rubbing her left wrist. "*Why* am I not permitted here? Is it *you* to say whether or not I am permitted here?"

The Nephilim set her down gently to the ground, and she howled in pain as she put even the tiniest fraction of weight on her left ankle. Although it did not appear to be broken, she had twisted it badly and would not be able to walk.

"No, it is not *I* who says you are not permitted here," he said, looking at her with concern, not receiving any kind of guidance on the words he should speak, which was a bit surprising given his proximity to the Trees.

He was gazing in the direction of the Trees, and Eve turned to see what he was looking at, understanding intuitively that this was part of the answer to her question. As she looked at the Trees, she again felt full of emotion, but was able to rein it in now.

"Who … *what* are they?" Eve asked with some confusion. "It is *who*, isn't it? Those are not ordinary trees …" she said plainly.

"You are the first human to look upon Yahweh and Baal," the Nephilim said, kneeling down to bring his face closer to Eve's, and to watch her more carefully as she stood on one foot at the precipice.

"Which one is Yahweh?" she asked, unwilling to let the conversation return to the part about her lacking permission to be there.

For his part, he did not press. "Yahweh is at the base of the valley, drinking deeply, directly, water from the lake, opening Its branches into the air," he replied, "And Baal is springing out of the earth, and Its roots go deeply into this mountain, deeply enough to feel the warmth of the fire inside …"

"Why do I feel so *strange* looking at these Trees?" she asked, still unable to comprehend her feelings, eyes still moist, but now it was clear to her that it had been the *Trees* filling her with a calm and a desire to remain south of here, and *still* she felt the push to go back. Yet, as before, this push fell short of a *command*. Was the command now coming from her tall, glowing acquaintance?

The Nephilim was seeking any indication that he was or was *not* allowed to talk to her about how he understood things.

"I feel it all but impossible to tell you," he said, "In *words*, I mean. You have to understand that I have only known words for three or four weeks, but I have lived here for many, *many*, of your lifetimes.

"Although to be honest, my memory is not very sharp, as my form was altogether different just a *month* ago, and *very* different twenty years earlier, one *hundred* years earlier, five *million* years earlier …"

Eve sensed what the word 'hundred' had meant but his word 'million' did not register, so she just took it to mean some amount greater than one hundred.

"In regard to our forms, I can tell you that Yahweh and Baal are responsible for that. I believe that in a very real sense Yahweh and Baal created me, created *us* – look carefully, and you will see many more Nephilim below, and not all of them resemble humans yet –" he said, pointing below.

A slight feeling of vertigo mixed with the swell coming from the majestic Trees had caused Eve to hobble back slowly from the edge, finding it utterly natural to lean against the kneeling Nephilim's thigh, putting her head against his – its – stomach.

"It has only been in conversations with you and with Mehujael that I have begun wondering whether everything I see has come from Yahweh and Baal, or if only it is the things that move and *grow*. I know that they are to me like you and Adam are to *Cain* …"

Hearing the names of Adam and Cain brought a small feeling of shame to Eve's breast. It was made difficult by the apparent fact that her mind and heart were not entirely own, that it was somehow possible to fill the mind with thoughts from the outside, that *trees* for pity's sake could flood her heart with emotions, or enhance the emotions already there …

It was nearly overwhelming, but she could not help but feeling the most powerful love she had ever felt as she felt the skin of the Nephilim beside her and watched the intertwined Trees in the distance, buffeted slightly by a wind, full of fruit.

"Since my first encounter with you I have had … *conversations* … with Baal and with Yahweh …" he said, "Conversations that do not involve words and that would be impossible to convert *into* words. But I do understand that I exist to *serve*, exist only at their pleasure. I am not … *permitted* … otherwise."

Eve turned now to look at the Nephilim and felt a profound sadness.

"Perhaps you *are* permitted to do and be otherwise," she said. "As I walked here, I was fighting an instinct that told me I was supposed to remain with Michael and Gabriel and your brethren, with my tribe. I know that it was coming from *this valley*, and I chose to *ignore* the instinct because it was not mine."

"Perhaps that is something *you* can ultimately choose to do," the Nephilim said, considering what she had said and beginning to feel nagging doubts fill his mind.

"You are not directly their creation as *I* am. I am their eyes and *ears*, their hands and legs and *wings* in this world. I am meant to do their bidding, feel as they *want* me to, behave as they will *have* me behave …"

Eve considered this and felt dissatisfied.

"Did you say '*Gabriel*'?" he asked her.

"Yes – the five Nephilim who came to us last night were meant to be named by Adam. Adam has understood for some weeks that it is *he* who must give things names. What was once a pastime for Adam as we wandered the Earth is now his *duty*, he feels," she said, "But you did not want Adam to give you a name …"

In that moment she grew somewhat confused. Without words the Nephilim regarded her fixedly, and felt like he understood her thoughts and what she would say next.

"It was intended that Adam name *me*, yes," he said with dawning comprehension. She did not need to say anything further. "Intended by Yahweh and Baal, and I know that I am supposed to have a name. I do not know why, but it is what I am *supposed* to do."

"But you have chosen *not* to do what you are supposed to do," Eve said as an unbidden shiver went up her back. Behind her she could feel the wind pick up, hear leaves rustle with more force, and felt as if the mountain itself had shaken in a slight tremor, but that was surely her imagination.

●

"Surely her imagination," Alisha said sleepily and with a smile, "Nice touch."

Leph smiled a bit, unapologetic. "Shall I return in the morning and tell you the rest of the story?" he asked.

She nodded with closed eyes, her eyebrows furrowing somewhat, "Is it too early for there to be news of my husband?"

"I believe so," Leph said with undisguised sadness, "I still cannot believe that Talmai went there, that *he* was allowed to go there ... not that anyone could stop him. Perhaps *I* should be there as well ..."

Alisha's eyes sprang open. "*No*, Leph. *None* of us should be there. Not *one* of us will be in Sokoh ever again," she said. "*Believe* me – I am counting the hours till the Anakim have departed from that city and from that entire *world*. Let us have a century or two to gain some perspective, and maybe it will become clearer how we will save those children from themselves."

Part 3

Chapter 19

Javan had spent three full hours in contact with colleagues in Mount Carmel and Fantale, cobbling together a roster and an itinerary. Given the propensity of the Anakim for playing the long game, the stress Javan underwent was, to say the least, novel.

At two in the morning a truck emblazoned with Mountain Dew logos departed from a rendezvous point between an abandoned warehouse and a grove of thick trees, the nearest functioning light source hundreds of meters away.

The truck contained rapidly tapped Homikim resources in Qatar, to include two engineers, a locksmith, a pair of Doha policemen, and a professional lounge singer who had gained expertise in explosives while attached to the Royal Saudi Armed Forces. Each had been issued a sleek tranquilizer gun with five darts.

Javan regarded Bill Majors through the dim, who ran his fingers carefully over his gun, avoiding an inadvertent disabling of the safety mechanism. Supplied by Raoul, there had been some mention that the contents of the cartridges were sourced from Tacaná, another blatant – and successful – attempt to pique Javan's interest in his backstory.

This he mentally shelved forcibly, focusing on the numbers assembled by Mohammed Al-Qamrun four days earlier – less than two days before perishing in a house fire – transmitted via secure ftp that had hit five Internet and two Undernet routers before being received in Fantale, where it sat aside the regular reports Mohammed had submitted each month during his five years employed by Al Jazeera in Doha.

There would be between six and eight people in the building. Javan had an appreciation of their schedules and locations, to include personal habits, which Mohammed had ascertained by secreting hours of internal security footage home on VHS tapes he restored to infrequently opened cabinets the following day.

There were no cameras in the poorly-lit parking lot to the south of the building, so the last camera that had captured the truck in transit was part of the municipal system, recording its passage with abysmal resolution.

Two Homikim left the cab, doors opened with gingerly, while the occupants of the specially-modified cargo space unbuckled themselves from seats fastened to the walls, and moved to exit the vehicle after parting a black curtain and lifting the rear door.

Entrance into the building was ultimately gained without an actual need for the locksmith, other than for his ability to open an unlocked door. Under the cover of night, Javan and Lemuel dispensed with the burqas, entering the Al Jazeera headquarters behind the team of Homikim.

Their easy ingress was due to security guards desiring an easy path to outside smoke breaks one could set their watch to. The retinue knew the placements of cameras throughout the building, and knew that security in the building was ridiculously lax.

Furthermore, Mohammed had years earlier added functionality to the security system that would be of great help, devoting an hour every month to ensure the additional features he had added remained in place, remained functional, and had not been discovered.

Such back doors were common when such devices came from security providers whose owners and whose lead engineers had blood ties to the Anakim, examples of which could be found on six continents.

The camera in the hallway they first entered was malfunctioning, something that had been effected months earlier by an avid smoker, and not by Mohammed. The present company knew this, and it gave them immediate, unobserved access to a simple keypad on the first floor of the Headquarters.

A Homikim named Mamoud entered a ten-digit code that gave him a one-line menu with three symbols most humans would not recognize. Within five minutes most of the cameras in the building were looping in a seamless manner, no longer recording anything new, and pressing the star key thrice on any given keypad would allow entrance into the controlled area beyond.

Bill Majors and the explosives expert led the party quickly to a room fifty yards from the door they had entered. Generally referred to as the Green Room, Al Jazeera had modeled theirs after those used by most New York City television studios.

Guests could be made comfortable here, and though the matter was open to some debate, this is where Javan and Lemuel did their level best at making their own large frames comfortable. The sight of a refrigerator caused Lemuel's stomach to rumble audibly, and he debated for several minutes whether anyone at Al Jazeera would notice food intended for guests having gone missing.

A Homikim named Calvin, one of the two engineers, had been appointed as the leader of the non-Anakim on this mission. He directed Bill to guard the door to the Anakim and make sure immediate needs were met.

According to Mohammed, there was absolutely no protocol for an external check-in with security during the evening. Doha was an affluent city, and policemen were well compensated for driving by the Headquarters once an hour, but they did not take the simple precaution of physically entering the building and speaking to a familiar face.

That being the case, Calvin and Mamoud and the entire party began fanning out around the building, focusing on rooms in which security guards were posted when not in motion (and if consistent, they wouldn't be until a smoke break at 3 a.m., and *maybe* for rounds at 4 a.m., if they felt up to a walk then).

One by one, doors were opened with care, whistling projectiles found their way into necks as heads turned at noises, and not one of the three guards dispatched was able to react before a heavy tranquilizer immediately caused vision to blur, and blurred vision swiftly followed by unconsciousness.

The skilled dart gun wielders produced red epi pens with identical cartridges that would provide these adult men an additional two hours of slumber.

A sweep of the building was complete by 2:40 a.m., with a final tally of four guards and two janitors snoring in a chemical haze at various points around the building. Jamal, a policeman during the day in a suburb of Doha, continued sweeping the building.

Mamoud remained in one of the security control rooms next to a sleeping guard, reestablishing the camera monitoring, but keeping all recording of video and audio offline. A variety of scanners of emergency bands were kept on, and he patched a special line to a contact in Mount Carmel, relaying an update in cryptic phrases over the insecure line.

Ali, the locksmith, had returned to the Green Room to signal that the Headquarters now belonged to them, for all intents and purposes. It was time for the *Anakim* to bring their expertise to bear, and that meant it was showtime for Lemuel.

They walked with heads lowered down a stretch of hallways until they found themselves in the largest control room in the building, openly connected with a series of studio set pieces, from which the anchorpeople delivered the news and weather daily.

Lemuel made his way past several editing booths and the panels devoted to live broadcasting, with levers that performed fades and cuts between the studio cameras, accessing videotapes housed in slots here and elsewhere in the building, or taking in streams coming from various satellites, or from other stations sending devoted feeds.

Though most things were labeled carefully, Lemuel searched the area for a full concordance, finding it among a stack of instruction manuals and blueprints and maps that showed the source and destination of every wire.

On this score, Mohammed had been less thorough in his intelligence, but this was precisely why Lemuel was there in person. It was a secondary vocation that allowed him to keep the entire collective of the Anakim interconnected, and to keep information from the human world flowing into their underground cities.

As he laid out a series of documents that Javan could not make heads nor tails of, Lemuel's finger quickly traced several paths, coming to a point on a blueprint that caused him to whirl around and march back into the nearest hallway.

"Javan!" he said, "With all likelihood the feed from Baghdad would have been recorded in *that* room 30 feet down the hall, on the right." They walked to the room with their small entourage and Lemuel punched two stars into the keypad, unlocking the door to a room containing banks of videotape recorders.

The racks of recorders were better labeled than the control panels in the room they had just left, and they found a recorder that appeared to be devoted to incoming direct feeds from Baghdad. There were three videotapes lying on top of the machine, labeled with date ranges for late March and early April of 2003, about a week in each range.

The most recent range ended on the 6th of April, which was the day before the incident at the Museum in Baghdad. Lemuel and Javan, heads bent low, gave each other a quick look and both inhaled deeply. Javan's hand came slowly up to the video recorder, and his thick finger moved to the hinged rectangle that would cover an inserted videotape, nudging it slowly inward.

The rectangle found no purchase until it had been nudged against the top of the machine. Javan did not need to peer inside to know it was empty, but he inserted his Anakim hand as far as it would go to verify what he already knew to be the case.

"Son of a *Yeti*!" he spat. He withdrew his hand and the two Anakim began to consider what their next move would be.

Lemuel did not hesitate. "It is possible that someone neglected to put in a new tape to replace the one that filled up on April 6th. Or this tape was mislabeled and kept in past the date it says …" Lemuel said, producing from his pocket a small electronic device he activated, sliding it up and down each of the three Baghdad tapes they had found.

"The likeliest scenario, given that Baghdad is currently the hottest spot in the entire Middle East, is that the Al Jazeera people have been *diligent* in monitoring whatever comes from Baghdad, and the tape was taken somewhere else for viewing."

It was Javan's turn to talk. "Without getting into details, we have kept some tabs on the communications of intelligence organizations around the world, and naturally, we have Homikim in nearly all of them. We have no indication that any Qatar communications intercepted *anywhere* have contained the phrase 'Jesus *flensing* Christ, someone get me the Chicago Bulls recruiters on the phone!'" Javan said, searching Lemuel for any sense that a joke he had worked on for a solid ten minutes while on the jet to Doha had landed.

He found no such sign, and cleared his throat forcefully.

"*No* private communications indicate distress or surprise … not that we are anywhere near all-reaching and all-knowing, but our hypothetical scenarios on what *would* happen if there were such a serious breach do not match what we are witnessing in the world in the last 36 hours."

"But it seems pretty inconceivable that no one looked at that tape," Lemuel proposed.

"I agree," Javan said. "And so we have perhaps two, perhaps three hours now to do a room-by-room sweep of the premises."

He held up the small mobile communication devices Raoul had given them, encrypted with algorithms designed by Anakim mathematicians. "Keep in touch, everyone. Bill, you memorized the layout of the building. Give assignments to all of us, including Lemuel and myself."

With that, they parted company and began star-star-starring their way into every office, bathroom, dressing room, and equipment shelter, looking at any stray videotape they encountered.

Unable to help himself, Lemuel used his device to wipe clean every single tape he came across, even though he was fairly certain the one they sought would have been kept properly labeled by whoever had viewed it.

Nearing the end of a series of rooms in a basement hallway, he found himself perplexed to find the last room appearing to be lit from inside. He skipped a few dark rooms and made a beeline to the translucent rectangle of light, adrenalin coursing through his entire system.

He pressed star star star and flung open the door to find an office with, among many other things, a single paper-strewn desk, a single velour chair behind the desk. In the chair was a human who had not been part of their crew.

Lemuel dropped his magnetic device and began fumbling for the tranquilizer gun at his side. The man jumped up, causing papers to fly in all directions and shouted, "Whoa! Wait! *Wait!* Are you *Javan* or are you *Lemuel*?"

Chapter 20

Goliath had spent nearly a full minute staring at General Rihab, who returned the stare without any sign of discomfort or fear. There were plenty of things unspoken and Goliath chose to make an educated guess for those things and leave it at that.

Clearly the Philistines were unhappy that there were not more Anakim there to make this contest more interesting, even though they had all agreed that Saul would be allowed to take Sokoh within the week.

If they were not going to provide more support, they had no *right* to demand the Philistines abide by the plan they had laid out to the letter. This was a matter of pride, after all. To just let the Israelites come take this crown jewel in the hills? This formerly Anakim city? *Unacceptable.*

Or so Goliath surmised, and Goliath had grown astute at reckoning the narrow thinking that these Philistine military men displayed. He turned his gaze to the two farm boys, barely old enough to shave, blood nearly done clotting in streaks down their faces, gathering in the knots that bound their wrists.

"May I take these two prisoners for questioning?" Goliath asked. Ozem would have looked more terrified, had he any more strength with which to do so. David looked resigned.

"Will you bring them back to me?" Rihab asked with his back to Goliath, having turned to look at the map of Sokoh and its environs, now modified to incorporate the recent intelligence update.

"*Must* I?" Goliath asked, seeing no purpose to having taken them prisoner in the first place. Was the intent to get to this Jesse, and through Jesse to get to King Saul?

Ozem found the strength *now* to regard Goliath with great trepidation. This giant did *not* intend to bring them back alive, surely seeing no use for hostages.

The generals as one looked at Goliath, clearly indicating their expectation.

"Just take *that* one," Rihab said, "You don't need to question both."

Goliath mentally kicked himself for his unwise backtalk. He had fully intended to release both of them, and now would be hard-pressed to release this youngest prisoner without annoying the Philistine military leaders. Further, he noted that both brothers looked distraught at being separated, so he decided not to prolong the separation and gently took David by the arm, motioning him to accompany him.

They walked in silence, Goliath taking the same route he had recently walked with Simon and Kenaz, heading directly for the Temple of Life.

They had not gone thirty yards from the courtyard when Goliath prompted David to stop, unsheathing his sword. David inhaled quickly and immediately berated himself for betraying fear. Goliath deftly sliced through David's bonds and said, "It's only five minutes from here."

David rubbed his wrists and stared up at Goliath suspiciously. Goliath held a torch in his left hand, and there were torches now lit at regular intervals along these streets, part of a laborious effort to convince the Hebrew army that the city contained ten times the number of soldiers than in fact it did.

The twilight was dark enough that David would have had *some* chance had he took off running then and there. His hands now unbound and ten seconds having gone by, he decided that the optimal times to run were eight seconds ago – and some unforeseeable time in the future.

After all, there was Ozem to consider, and there was nothing lost by listening to what this Anakim, the first to whom he had *ever* spoken, was going to ask him.

They reached the Temple of Life, and Goliath was happy to see that there was light coming from within, meaning that Talmai was still there, and waiting for him to visit.

They walked through the expansive front entrance, open to the outside air, up to a wall six feet beyond which could be circumvented either to the left or to the right. Goliath and David went around to the right and entered the main chamber of the Temple, and both were somewhat astonished by what they saw.

In the days since Goliath had last met Talmai in the Temple, Talmai had stocked the pit with kindling and sticks and wood and this evening had a healthy fire going. A sole goblet remained on the altar in the back of the chamber, surrounded by three short vials of liquids and a large container of red wine.

David sensed that Talmai was at least twice as old as the oldest man he had ever seen, and if rumors were true, perhaps even older than that. Talmai smiled broadly at both of them and motioned for them to sit on benches designed to comfortably hold even a tall Anakim, 12 or 13 feet tall.

"And whom have you brought with you tonight, Goliath?" Talmai asked, taking a seat across the fire pit from where Goliath sat and David perched. David felt seven years old again, given how large the bench was in comparison to his body.

"My name is David," he said somewhat defiantly, though he found his rancor tempered by what appeared to be a good-natured, elderly person that custom demanded he treat with extreme deference. "I believe that I am prisoner of the Philistines and of the Anakim."

Talmai frowned at this, saying, "You might be a prisoner of the Philistines but I *assure* you, you are *not* a prisoner of the Anakim."

Goliath shot Talmai a bit of a look and Talmai ignored the look with a deftness that had taken centuries to hone. This kind of dismissal was an unsubtle nudge to any Anakim who had not yet reached Emancipation.

"Perhaps we need to assess who this young man is *before* we make that sort of determination, Talmai," Goliath said, unconvincingly.

"And who *are* you, young man?" Talmai asked. He rested his chin on his left fist and stared at David, slight lines of worry undisguisable in the light of the flickering flames.

David could not help thinking about his sisters left at the farmstead, about his older brothers who had marched on Sokoh this very day. The thought of his brothers needing him caused his stomach to turn to steel. He swallowed, drew himself up somewhat, and for the first time in fifteen minutes thought of Michal, wanting desperately to live to see her again.

"I work on a farm three hours' walk west of here," David said, "I tend sheep. My father is Jesse, son of Obed, son of Boaz, all of us sons of *Judah*, sons of *Abraham*."

"Indeed?" Talmai said, looking over at Goliath with raised eyebrows. "If I am not mistaken, I was good friends with Boaz's great-grandfather, Aminadab, a long time ago …"

"I have a brother named Abinadab …" David said.

"Close enough," Talmai said with a short laugh. "Aminadab was the great-grandson of Judah himself, he said … or perhaps I am missing a generation. It has been a long time since I have been directly involved in the affairs of the Hebrew peoples …"

Talmai got up and walked to the altar, reaching towards a shelf behind the altar and returning with three goblets smaller than the goblet sitting atop. He poured red wine for each of them. "David, this comes from leagues east of here and it is *quite* fine. Do you enjoy wine with your dinners at home?"

David looked to his right at Goliath, who had all but given up keeping a stern look on his brow. He turned to find two goblets being held out towards him. One he passed to Goliath and the other he held in a slightly trembling hand.

Talmai returned with the remaining goblet to his seat, taking a long sip and smiling with broad satisfaction.

"It comes from a vineyard I had a hand in creating two hundred years ago, and this was a fine, fine year for those grapes," he said, "Now tell me, David, what do *you* think about this conflict between the Israelites and the Philistines?"

David brought the goblet up to his lips and took a slow, deliberate, small drink. It tasted quite fine indeed, and he followed with a longer sip, trying to clear cobwebs from his throbbing head.

He could not help but trust this older Anakim immediately, and he had had enough time sitting next to Goliath, observing his body language in his peripheral vision, that his gut instinct was causing his guard to begin to lower itself. The wine would complete the lowering of said guard.

"My brother Abinadab and my father said they used to come to Sokoh twenty years ago and had *no* fear of Anakim," David began. "But it is the will of *Yahweh* that brought Saul here. These lands all once belonged to Jacob and to Judah."

"With all due respect," Talmai said, speaking in a tone David felt in his heart was respectful, "These lands never *belonged* to Jacob, nor to Judah. These lands contained many peoples, my own included."

David had little to say to this. Talmai clearly had years on him. Still, he couldn't help but ask, "You were alive back then in the time of Judah? You know this to be true?"

"You impudent *pup!*" Goliath roared to David's right, causing David nearly to drop his goblet. Talmai had felt a hint of annoyance, but this outburst caused him to let out a hearty cackle.

"Goliath, understand that I am sharing this hearth with *two* impudent pups," Talmai said.

"No, David. My *father* was alive then and knew Judah. There are still Anakim living today who knew Judah, and were they *here*, they could tell you that themselves and answer your questions. I'm afraid that I cannot offer knowledge or experiences I do not possess."

David forced himself to slow down his consumption of the wine, which he was drinking quickly out of nervousness. The nervousness was beginning to wane, thanks to the wine, and David was hazily unsure this was wise.

"I believe it is the contention of Saul that it is the *clear* will of Yahweh that we possess all of these lands, whether or not we did back in the time of Judah," David said, looking around the Temple and finding himself full of questions he hoped he had the time to ask.

"I must admit, I don't understand why we are fighting to possess a city that was built for Anakim. There seems to be plenty of room for *Anakim* cities and for *human* cities – cities for Israelites and cities for Philistines. I'm not sure I understand why Saul is doing this."

"But I believe you just said that it was *Yahweh* who directed Saul to take Sokoh," Goliath said. "Or does Yahweh speak to you directly?"

David's cheeks burned bright red, though he wasn't quite sure why. Goliath was echoing the calm tone of Talmai rather than in the harsher tones of the Philistine soldiers.

He took the question at face value and answered, "No, I do *not* speak to Yahweh directly. But my family keeps the covenant our people established with Yahweh at the time of Moses. If we are faithful, Yahweh will continue to bless our people with happiness and abundant food and water."

"Do you feel that killing other peoples and taking their cities is necessary to be happy?" Goliath asked.

David again felt the dueling forces of anger and calm. This felt very much like his conversations with his brother Shammah, who could say things David disagreed with strongly but in a way such that David did not feel directly attacked – just his ideas attacked, and there was a *safety* in ideas being attacked when there was respect in a conversation.

So – this was not an *Eliab* conversation. Not an *Ozem* conversation. A *Shammah* conversation, and that's how David would regard it from now on. His shoulders relaxed. He took another drink, nearly finishing the goblet.

"There are matters in which I don't believe it is for *me* to decide," David said. "I tend sheep. I must look to my father to dictate what I should do when I am *not* tending sheep. And my father looks to our *king*, looks to *Saul*, to determine what our family does to serve our people.

"Perhaps it is Samuel now who holds the ear of the king with regard to the dictates of Yahweh. But I know that I ignore the dictates of Yahweh at my own peril, at the peril of my family and of my people."

David finished his goblet of wine.

Goliath had finished his by then and took Talmai's lead in how this interrogation would play out. He got up, took the flask of wine, restored everyone's goblet, returned to his seat.

"Your family does not worship Baal," Talmai stated, asked. David cringed slightly from the mention, and hearing the name Baal helped restore his wariness and brought his guard back up a little.

"My family does not worship Baal. Yahweh has demanded that there be no god before him," David said.

Talmai smiled at this. "Do you think Yahweh minds if some of your people worship Baal as well as Yahweh, as long as Yahweh retains prominence?" he asked, sincerely.

David considered this, knowing that indeed, other farmers a day or two north of their homestead did *precisely* that, praising Baal for good crops, performing certain rituals to ensure the crops remained good.

"Samuel assures us that only Yahweh is worthy of our worship and will provide for all our needs. Baal is a *false* god ..." David said, pausing to drink some wine and ponder this.

"This is important, David," Talmai said, "Is Baal a *false* god ... or does Baal not exist *at all*? Is there *truly* a Yahweh who provides for you? What do you think?"

"I *do* believe in Yahweh," David said without hesitation. "I do not doubt that Yahweh has rewarded my family for its devotion, and will continue to do so if we remain faithful. I understand that the Anakim view things differently."

Talmai nodded thoughtfully.

"The Anakim are faithful in much the same way the humans are faithful," Talmai said. "What we believe to be true must ultimately be decided by each individual – after having been brought up in our communities, educated, having walked the Earth to gain experience ..."

"And then you walk through the fire?" David asked, repeating a phrase he had heard from Shammah. Something Talmai had said had triggered David's memory.

Goliath shot a look at Talmai, who didn't react to the look or to the phrase.

"Yes. We Walk through the Fire," Talmai said, emphatically, "It is one of many ceremonies in the lives of the Anakim and of the humans who walk among us. Indeed, this Temple of Life has seen many of these ceremonies in the past three centuries …"

"Some humans …" David said wistfully, knowing how excited Shammah would be if he were there, engaged in this conversation.

"You mean …" and David knew what he was about to say was rude, but he did not know of a euphemism to soften it, "*Half-breeds?*" Goliath buried his face in his right hand, wanting to take this lad over his knee and spank the adolescence out of him.

"The *Homikim*," Talmai said. "These are not *mules*, David. You should not use that hateful word again."

David looked genuinely chastened. "I didn't *know* any other word, sir," he said in a penitent tone.

"It has been a long time since Israel sent ambassadors … humans that are *not* Homikim … to live with the Anakim and vice versa," Talmai said. "Much has been forgotten by your people. You do know that some of your patriarchs were extremely long-lived …"

"Are you saying that Abraham was Homikim?" David asked, implications immediately flooding his mind.

Talmai merely smiled at his. David turned to Goliath, who took a drink of wine and raised his right eyebrow in agreement.

David took a long pull and finished his second goblet of wine.

"So that would mean that all of *us* have Anakim blood running through our veins … and that makes *me* Homikim too, many generations removed, perhaps, but Homikim nonetheless," David said after a moment of deliberation, in ignorance.

Goliath stood up and stretched his legs.

"I would like to Walk through the Fire," David said, and Goliath felt his legs buckle slightly.

"Here, *now*, in this Temple. Will you perform the ceremony on me?"

Chapter 21

The Nephilim sat at the precipice looking at the tendrils of Yahweh embracing those of Baal, the tendrils of Baal embracing those of Yahweh.

Eve was nestled against him, finding the breeze cool enough to require external body heat to keep her warm. Her ankle had begun to throb, a pain that was beginning to spread to her head, and after a half day's travel that morning, she found herself falling asleep while the Nephilim pondered their last discussion – a discussion they had had in front of his presumed creators, in front of his sole reason for existence.

Surely obedience was required of him, of *all* the Nephilim. How could he explain having a desire not only independent of the Trees but not in *accordance* with the wishes of the Trees?

And yet now that he sat and thought on this, these independent feelings had begun from the moment they had changed him some weeks ago, and had sent him back to the humans.

His mind had been *empty* when he had been given sustenance from the Trees and sent forth, and that mind was a sponge that had absorbed much from the people he met, through conversations, through shared goals, through simple silent companionship, watching a large gold disk by day, a silver disk in the night sky and not understanding their natures.

The actions of the human beings seemed far divorced from the directives he received from the center of Eden, and he had taken a piece of that divorcement and had planted it as a seed in his heart.

When he noticed that Eve was asleep, he could not bring himself to rouse her. He knew that Baal and Yahweh did not wish her to be there, for *any* of the humans to be there, but he felt no drive to expel her from their midst.

Surely she could regain her strength first, as humans required. He looked down as her chest rose and fell against his, opened his consciousness to experience in a focused manner, savored the feel of her long, black, tangled hair against his bare skin.

The skin he wore was not inured from injury. There had been challenges from a variety of animals over the ages, things he half-remembered, and there had been times necessitating the Nephilim to return to their creators for repair.

An idea formed in his mind, and he had no good way to evaluate it without input from the Trees. He found that either executing the idea or going to get proper input required him to travel to the Trees, so he set in his mind to do so.

He stood up supporting Eve's weight carefully, listening to the tenderness of her hot breath. She did not awaken. And though he could begin to take her back to her people, this would not help her injuries. Not in the same way the *Trees* would be able to, he believed.

So he began gingerly stepping along the top of the canyon to his left, away from the river, circling towards the foothill that would lead up to where Baal sprang from a tiny mountain.

A direct approach to the base of Baal would be difficult, but the top of the canyon near Baal led to a path one could take down into the canyon, towards the lake at the bottom, towards the gigantic trunk of Yahweh.

As he grew closer, his mind finally began to receive vibrations of communication and direction from the Trees. There was a general acknowledgment of his action, a clear understanding that an unconscious human was being delivered unto them, a clear understanding of his desire that she be healed, having recently suffered physical trauma to her ankle and to her wrist, and he was made to understand that she could sleep here while Yahweh and Baal conferred privately.

After which he would almost *surely* be directed to return her to her people with maximal haste.

Their thoughts then left his mind to engage in a conferral to which he would not be privy, to which he had never been privy, to which he would never *be* privy.

He watched Eve sleep and he could feel ... *feel* ... a formerly-dormant enhancement to his understanding that had been made when Baal and Yahweh had changed his *mind*, had made him *bipedal* ... he felt deep warmth flushing his face.

He had unbidden hypothetical thoughts which troubled him. Imagined the trees coming awake, branches moving down to swirl around Eve's body (though the branches had never moved like that and perhaps *could not* move like that), crushing the life out of her and …

And he would not allow it. He would *not allow that.*

And he felt shame and confusion, and he gingerly ran the upper third of his right index finger alongside her cheek, inadvertently waking her up. She blinked a few times, confused about where she was, then saw the face of the Nephilim hovering above her and smiled as if she had naturally gone from experiencing this closeness while asleep, then awake.

She slowly directed his large hand down the side of her face, neck, across her breasts, across her stomach, and she suddenly recognized that her thoughts and feelings were part of an *ocean* of Thoughts and Feelings, and she *felt* where she was then, and there were Words in her head that were *not* words, and she did *not* understand them, but she suddenly remembered being born, remembered her first kiss, the first time a man entered her, and she knew what it would be to die, to cease breathing – all of this hitting her between heartbeats, and she thought she might burst.

And the Nephilim was given the same sensations, as if he were at the base of Yahweh, and he knew he was experiencing a communion – a communion he had not initiated, nor had Eve initiated, and the initiation could only have *one* source, but at that moment he did not want to devote a single fiber of his being to thoughts concerning *anything* other than this communion.

He had lain next to Eve and had pressed her body to his. In his mind he saw the entire valley full of people, men and women and hundreds, thousands of children, swimming, running, talking, eating, living.

In his mind he saw many lands – he saw vast stretches of water, sandy stretches where nothing lived, he saw frozen water and blinding freezing rain whipped by strong wind, and in all of these places he could see nations of people walking.

Tears were once more running down her cheeks and she felt a clenching in her loins, a tension that released into a paroxysm of joy, then returned, then released again, and this was an echo of the sensations she had had with Adam in their tent the night before – perhaps not an echo but rather its foretelling.

What she had felt with Adam was an echo of what she was *now* experiencing, and she loved Adam in that moment more deeply than she thought possible, as well as her sons, and Mehujael, and Siroc, and Mirab ... and this love extended to the animals they sometimes kept with them as companions, and beyond to *all* animals, *all* plants, everything on and under and above the Earth ...

Something inside her *turned*, then, and in her mind she understood that Cain and Abel would have a brother or a sister in less than four seasons, and understood that although she and Adam had been together recently, it was only because of the communion she was currently experiencing that this life had been created.

The Nephilim broke from her, breathing hard, not truly understanding what had just happened or why, but had experienced most of what Eve had experienced. He could not think straight. He had no *desire* to think straight.

For her part, Eve was ravenous. She walked stiffly, but with far less pain than before, towards a red apple at the edge of the lake, in the grass.

She took a large bite from it, her mind flashing on the recent ... *congress* ... with the Nephilim – how *else* could she think of it? – and feeling weak in the knees.

She walked back to the Nephilim who likewise seemed silent and contemplative and more than a little spent, and she gathered a few green and red apples along the way.

Eve held out one of the red apples to the Nephilim, who took it from her with a warm smile. Although he had watched humans eat with curiosity, he had also watched the inevitable consequence of ingesting sustenance in such forms, and the curiosity had not been strong enough to push him to determine how alike the bodies given them by Baal and Yahweh were to those of the humans ...

Eve had begun munching on a green apple now, and she was revisited by *every* conversation she had ever had in her entire life, could see again *every* performance ever put on by Mirab and Zillah, and she eagerly took a second bite.

The wind picked up, and dark clouds were flitting through the air. There was a change in pressure that both Eve and the Nephilim noticed, and as he worked his way through his second apple he suddenly thought of the source of the apples and felt panic enter his system, pushing aside all wellness.

It was a relief that Baal and Yahweh appeared to remain engaged in their own communion. He sensed that the communion was coming to an abrupt end, and the Nephilim also sensed that they were no longer alone.

They had been sitting with Eve leaning against his arm, and then as if in a dream there was *Adam* approaching them from the top of the canyon, walking down the incline that had borne them down earlier.

Adam looked furious, and Eve had never seen this look on his face before.

Although both Eve and the Nephilim remained clothed, Adam could feel the electricity in the air and it would take someone far less intuitive not to see an intimacy shared by his wife and this large interloper.

No one said a word until Adam stood fifteen feet away from where they were reclined at the edge of the lake, another fifteen feet from the edge of Yahweh's trunk.

Adam's eyes were already full of tears, as he had felt the same way Eve had felt when first bursting into the clearing. As his eyes narrowed in anger, tears freed themselves and he said plainly, sharply, "Lucifer."

The Nephilim stood up as if he had been stung by a two-foot-tall bee. The air around him was charged, and in the distance he saw a flash of lightning. Five seconds later, a peal of thunder.

"I do not wish this," he said, lips fumbling over the language.

"Lucifer!" Adam shouted. "I name you *Lucifer*!"

At this, Lucifer felt Yahweh and Baal awaken to the events around them, and he felt the mountain begin to tremble.

Chapter 22

Lemuel pointed a tranquilizer gun at the chest of the human sitting behind the desk, placing a nontrivial amount of pressure on the trigger. He channeled his inner Javan and barked, "Who are you and *why* are you here? *Five seconds!*"

And how do you know my *name*, he thought, sifting through the possibilities. As the man began to open his mouth, Lemuel added a barked "*Wait!*"

With his free hand Lemuel fumbled for his two-way mobile device and pressed the broadcast button, enunciating crisply, "Attention, everyone. I've encountered someone our initial reconnaissance missed, and he asked me if I were Javan or Lemuel. I'm in the southern corridor on the basement level. I'm conducting a one-minute interview and will sedate him if I don't like what he says. Out."

The human appeared of Arab descent, perhaps in his late thirties, wearing an immaculate blue suit that was not something one would expect to see in a broadcasting facility at three in the morning. Lemuel motioned to him that it was time for him to start talking.

"Okay," he said, "But you should give me two or three minutes here." He looked nervous, but the exact tenor of the nervousness seemed just the slightest bit off to Lemuel.

"My name is Marid and I am *Homikim*," he said, "I'm here to *help* you. I'm surprised you weren't told that I would be here ... I've been working at Al Jazeera for only two months, so I might not have been included in the original list of resources you could tap ... your list is *nearly* current, but a few weeks dated."

Lemuel relaxed some, but aimed not to show it in his face. "Go on," he said.

"You're looking for the videotape containing the direct feed from Baghdad that shows two Anakim entering the Baghdad Museum through a nontraditional entrance – Javan and Lemuel – I presume that you are one of *them*, yes?" he asked, clearly seeking some kind of affirmation.

"It would not be prudent to sedate me before I tell you what I know about this videotape you seek, yes?"

That was certainly true. Lemuel raised the communication device to his mouth and said, "Subject claims to be a Homikim named Marid and is here with *sanction*. He knows why we're here. Check in with Carmel and I will find out more."

Four seconds later he heard a distant voice down the hallway that was Javan rapidly approaching, rapidly speaking into his more-tricked-out communication device, conversing with someone back home in Mount Carmel, finding out what he could about Marid.

"Why are you in this room? Have you *found* anything?" Lemuel asked. Marid had finished slowly gathering up the scattered papers and returned them to their original piles on top of the desk.

He kept his hands vaguely in an 'up' position, seemingly demonstrating that he wasn't going to reach for any kind of weapon, and he certainly didn't appear to be set to try to run past Lemuel and effect an escape.

Javan entered the room slowly, and Marid nodded at his entrance calmly.

"This is the office of Laith al-Khaled, a senior reporter for Al Jazeera. He writes copy for the talent – for those who read his words on the air, and his focus is on Iraq and Iran," Marid said.

"I'm also a reporter for Al Jazeera and Laith has become a *friend* of mine. This morning, eighteen hours ago, Laith ran into my room waving a videocassette and sweating profusely. It took him a few minutes to compose himself. I do not need to tell you what was on the tape.

"Clearly Baal is looking out for us – he brought the tape to *me*? No one *else*? I told him it looked extremely well crafted – had *he* manufactured it? Was it a joke gift for Omar's birthday next week? He gazed at me strangely, having not considered that what he had seen could be some cleverly-edited special effect. He asked me if that's what I thought it was, because it looked real to *him*.

"I allowed that if it *were* real, it was very important and that we needed to make a backup copy immediately, and I don't need to tell you I have already destroyed *that* copy. But clearly the best explanation of the tape was that it was an elaborate prank being played upon us in this extremely tense time with Americans invading sovereign Muslim territory …"

Javan had stepped to Lemuel's side, watching closely the man's posture and gestures, assessing the words as he assessed the person.

"I'm Marid," the man said, offering his hand to Javan, as Lemuel awkwardly stepped to the side. Lemuel had already put away his gun.

Javan warily took Marid's small hand in his and said, "I am Javan and this is Lemuel. Carmel has verified that you are Homikim and started working at Al Jazeera after the last time we centralized a Homikim census of employment here in Doha, Qatar. Will you come with us?"

Marid nodded enthusiastically. "I am done here – I was able to convince Laith to hold off on showing that tape to anyone else until it had been authenticated by our Photoshop and editing wizards, both of which were already gone for the day by the time Laith had made that decision," Marid said.

"I think we're looking at a best-case containment scenario here. I've been in every drawer, nook, and cranny in this room and the tape is *not* here. Laith must have taken it home with him. I would suggest we go there now."

"It shouldn't take more than twenty minutes for the others to complete their sweep of Al Jazeera and then we'll get back into our truck …" Javan said, looking at Lemuel, who was clearly taking this in and likewise wondering if they had hit such a lucky break that they could opt out of the mission at this point and just get back undercover until it was safe to complete a return journey to Mount Carmel.

Marid grabbed an envelope off of the desk and said, "This must be his address. Although I have become casual friends with Laith in the two months I've been here, I haven't been invited to his house yet. All I know about his home is that his wife's name is Adiba and he has two young daughters."

The two Anakim had already returned to the hallway, immediately grateful for the additional head room, and Marid followed them as they made their way to a staircase leading up to the entrance they had used to enter the building.

"If you don't mind my asking, what did you do with the other people here?" Marid asked, "I arrived here four hours ago – the guard I spoke to couldn't have been less interested in why I was coming in at eleven p.m. ..." He opened the door that led outside, holding it open for the two Anakim.

Javan answered, "They are all asleep and set in chairs. We administered sedatives that are slightly psychotropic. They will have strange dreams for the next few hours, and will awaken disoriented enough not to remember how they came to be asleep, and they are likely to feel a little ashamed that they did so.

"They are likely to compare notes and will be somewhat alarmed that the security cameras were disabled overnight, but we will be long gone by then. Rumors of a gas leak will be sent to executives of Al Jazeera mid-day tomorrow ..."

Marid stopped abruptly, shoe squeaking loudly, and Javan and Lemuel turned back to face him, and to watch for the rest of the company to join them in this dark parking lot. Javan caught a wisp of hostility in Marid's posture.

"Drugs. You gave them *drugs* to confuse them," Marid said through a narrowed mouth. "As you do for the Rite of Moloch."

Then, in the span of a second, calm and neutrality returned to Marid's facial features, but that was a second that did not just flit past Javan unobserved.

"They are similar to the substances most commonly used in the Rite of Moloch," Javan said with soft deliberation, "Though, as you know, the Rite is not the same everywhere, and every part of the Rite is voluntary."

Marid adopted a look of slight embarrassment. Behind him, Bill and Mamoud emerged from the Headquarters.

"I'm sorry about that outburst. I went *Through the Fire* in Alpenheim twenty years ago. I chose to ingest everything during the Rite, and I had a bad reaction to one of the extracts," Marid said in echoed restraint.

"I was sick for a week, and I elected to repeat the experience later, declining any chemical enhancements of the journey."

Lemuel watched his old friend raise an eyebrow and nod with understanding, knowing it to be a mask. He looked forward to when they could privately discuss the events of this outing, hoping for resolution to be had when they caught up with Laith al-Khaled.

Once assembled and debriefed, Marid stood casually with the other Homikim, as if he'd started out the evening with them on this excursion. The others were fitful, having enjoyed the novel excursion, and the unprecedented sight of simply standing in the open with two giants, but were starting to feel keenly vulnerable.

Javan allowed himself a few more seconds to bask in this rare recklessness and then took hold of the reins again.

Marid offered to lead them to the home of Mr. al-Khaled, which appeared to lie almost directly on the route between the Headquarters and Raoul's estate, but Javan directed Marid to accompany them in the cargo hold of the truck.

The gray and beige decal in Marid's windshield was identical to five other cars parked nearest the building in the mostly empty lot, and Marid's car would attract no attention.

While en route, Lemuel provided an interim briefing to Halakan in Alpenheim, and he knew the situation report would be rapidly disseminated to the entire support structure monitoring the situation. He found it awkward speaking to Javan's bakhatu for the very first time under this odd circumstance, but understood that Javan's undivided attention needed to be focused on the road before them, both literally and metaphorically.

"You believe he has the tape with him," Javan reiterated, breaking a minute of silence in which all assembled felt slightly claustrophobic in the tight quarters of the twelve-foot-long Mountain Dew cargo bay. His eyes continued to scan the streetlights and taillights ahead.

"This is the exit coming up," Bill muttered to Calvin from the passenger seat in the cabin, gesturing.

"It's the only thing that makes sense," Marid said. "These are not tapes that *anyone* has any reason to bring out of the building. Perhaps once a month a tape will drift into an editing booth somewhere for a story to be put together, after which the tape returns to storage. I checked all the booths, as I'm sure you did."

Lemuel massaged his right calf, as his legs were awkwardly folded so as to avoid other legs. He kept his eyes fixed on Marid, feeling that Javan would want him to, as Javan had seemingly spent the last twenty minutes choosing his words and gestures and facial expressions with more care than earlier that evening.

"I do not believe he has any means of digitizing that tape and uploading it to the Internet, but I've only been inside his house once," Marid said, and Javan registered the slightest constriction of the throat. Javan gave no response, but continued to stare through the aperture to the cabin, out the windshield of the truck.

"What would the contingency plan be if he did?" Marid asked. Mamoud stared up at Lemuel with wide eyes, wondering at the boldness of the question.

Lemuel waited a few seconds for Javan to speak, then elected to lean into a spontaneity he hoped Javan would follow and approve of.

"When you say 'upload to the Internet', it's a phrase that requires specifics before I could give you any genuine answer to the question," Lemuel said, his peripheral vision regarding Javan to his right. Lemuel found no sign that he should cease.

"Depending on his Internet provider … *assuming* the video made it past the virtual and physical networks *we* control … then we would likely copy what was broadcast and doctor it so that our version had subtle but deterministic marks of an ultra-expert fake."

"Flood the conspiracy theory billboards with it … alter timestamps … do our level best to ensure that our copy spreads just as rapidly as the original."

Lemuel let the implications settle. Every Homikim in the cargo bay listened with interest, he noted. He felt a slight boost with the attention, helping to assuage the knot in his stomach that grew with every hour that passed without finding a resolution to their mission.

They slowed down as they entered a densely-populated well-lit neighborhood, and within five minutes, Calvin was pulling the truck over to the side of the street.

"2502 was three houses back," Calvin said through the aperture that led to the back of the truck, "Tallest house on this block."

"That's pretty clever," Marid said, nodding thoughtfully in the near dark.

"There are lights on in the house," Bill Majors reported from the front, picking up a small set of binoculars to get a better look.

Javan ran his right hand through his beard. Lemuel saw this as a human affect Javan rarely employed. Javan was waiting for something.

"I could give him a call," Marid said. "He was pretty shook up today, and to be honest, *I* was as well. If I called him to say *I couldn't sleep, thinking about what you showed me today*, I don't believe it would be suspicious. Perhaps I could be invited over."

Lemuel touched Marid's shoulder, and Marid turned towards him. Lemuel reached into a pocket close to his heart, inside a vest, and produced a small electronic device.

"This will demagnetize any videotape you come across," Lemuel said, recognizing how far he was straying from the role he was meant to play … that is to say, if he were to *faithfully* follow the dictates of his avocation, and to only act when given direct and *explicit* guidance from Javan.

There were numerous ways Javan could have conveyed to Lemuel that this straying was unwelcome and counterproductive. Javan did not convey this to Lemuel.

"Mamoud, take the clipboard and perform some recon," Javan said, and the two Doha policemen at the back of the bay pulled aside the curtain, then lifted the well-oiled back of the truck just large enough for Mamoud to awkwardly lay down on the floor and slide out.

Mamoud brushed off dust from the Mountain Dew logo on his uniform, and he smiled at the thought of pretending to be confused and lost as he took the lay of their immediate vicinity.

Javan turned to his right and met Marid's eye, his eyesight for over seven decades honed to see clearly even in the dimmest of light.

"Make the call, Marid," Javan replied.

Chapter 23

"Remember, David, that what you will experience here today is only an *approximation* of the Rite of Moloch," Talmai said, standing behind the altar at the head of the Temple of Life, ten feet from where a fire pit roared with a healthy blaze.

Goliath continued to feed it with wood that Talmai had brought there in recent days. David sat cross-legged on the floor on the opposite side of the pit from the altar, and Goliath stood in front of a stone bench to David's left.

"Which is why we should not *do* this, Talmai," Goliath said in exasperation, "I can only give the advice of an Anakim not yet forty years after *his* Walk ... but I do not understand what can be gained by doing this."

"I am trying to appreciate the *path* upon which Saul has set our people. My entire family and my livelihood are impacted by what happens on the borders of these lands," David said, attempting to sound mature beyond his years.

He could only attempt this thanks to the hours he had spent with his sisters and Shammah and his father debating theology and discussing agriculture.

"I understand our relationship with the Philistines, but I feel like it might be vital that I understand the *Anakim* better. Approximation or not, I know that I will get *something* out of this ritual I might bring back to the rest of Israel."

Talmai finished pouring a tiny amount of pale blue liquid from a skin into the goblet that had been set in the center of the altar.

"David, will you willingly open your mind to *Baal*? Will you willingly open your mind to *Yahweh*? Will you drink this and take your first step into the *Fire*?" Talmai asked, using words that were almost identical to the ritual he had experienced three centuries earlier.

In contrast, these walls were bare and were not filled with representational works of art, and the room was not filled with other Anakim and Homikim there to guide the participant. In spite of this, Talmai's reverent words provided a splash of cold water thrown over Goliath's head, and his objections ended immediately.

In his mind's eye, Goliath could see a web of light encircling a forest, could hear his heart beat loudly inside his chest, could feel the naked fear that a newborn deer feels when confronted with his very first cold, gray day outside of the womb.

Talmai circled the pit to David and handed the goblet to him. David took the offered goblet and said, "I *will*" with conviction, baffled at the source of this conviction.

Part of his body still ached from the beating he had received seven hours earlier, but the ache was being replaced by a *drive* and by a *curiosity* he would not have been able to easily describe.

Did he *truly* mean to open his mind to *Baal*? As he brought the goblet to his lips and drank, a bitter taste nearly overwhelmed his tongue, causing tears to well up in his eyes. Would Yahweh forgive him if he were deliberately going astray?

Talmai took back the goblet and returned to his position behind the altar.

"David, what you just tasted is an extract that comes from plants that used to grow only near the river Euphrates," Talmai said, "We cultivate it on our own now, trusting that the liquid the plants produce shares the same properties as the liquid one would have obtained from its ancestors – which sprouted in the Cradle of Life we call *Eden*."

Goliath took a seat on the floor in front of the altar, through the flames, across from where David sat. He knew the role Talmai expected of him, and would sooner die than disrespect him.

"Look into the *flames*, David," he said, "I want you to think about fire, how it *destroys*, how it *purifies*, how it *takes* life, how it *preserves* life."

David looked into the flames and went through the list that Goliath had just outlined. The dual nature of fire was pretty obvious, and not something you would need to argue with anyone about, so David felt he was profoundly missing the point, or that perhaps the Anakim needed to work on their rituals.

It was at this point that he began to see tendrils of light extend, wave gracefully, from the ends of the leaves of flame in front of him. Through the fire he saw

Talmai become less distinct, less real, and he began to pay more attention to the fire itself.

His mind felt heavy with fog, and the flames of the fire seemed – *slower* – somehow. His mind drifted to thinking about Eden, and how far away Sokoh was from where the prophets thought Eden to be, and for the first time in his life he wondered how big the world actually was, and his mind tried to determine that – by *backing away* from the world until he could see it all.

The fire five feet in front of him was suddenly below him, and then he imagined that he had floated out of the building and could see the Temple of Life below him – pulling back further, he could imagine all of Sokoh, and begin to imagine the cities close to Sokoh.

Inside he felt his mind was becoming *one* with Yahweh, who spoke to *prophets* – still *speaks* to prophets – from the *sky*, all-seeing, all-knowing.

It was a fraction of a fraction of a fraction of how Yahweh would *perceive* the world, but while the flickering flames five feet in front of him continued to trace colored streaks across his eyes, he was seeing *under* the fire and *between* the fire …

His thoughts were becoming erratic and fragmented, and he simultaneously had urges to snap back completely into focus and return body and soul to the Temple of Life – and to let his thoughts escape all logic, dissipate beyond words and reason.

In front of him, an abstract appearance of the goblet – behind him, words from a voice he recognized, "David, now drink *this* extract – it is produced by trees we cultivate on the slopes of Mount Carmel. I want you to imagine that you are the very Earth itself, and I want you to imagine what it is to sustain the plants and trees who drive roots *into* you, seeking the water you keep *inside* of you …"

David had a sudden discordant thought that what he was doing, what he was being *asked* to do, was absurd. He took the goblet – yes, *those* were his hands, though he was somewhat alarmed at having to consciously understand that the hands he was looking at were actually connected to him – he began to sip from the goblet, tasting honey, and he had an odd sense he was drinking the *idea* of honey.

The liquid seemed to take ten minutes to travel every crook and crevice of his tongue – from his perch far above Sokoh, his mind returned for a split second into its rightful place.

He saw Goliath saunter to stand across from him, gazing at him fixedly, and behind Goliath the *altar*, and behind the altar *Talmai*, and behind Talmai he perceived an indistinct older, hunched over Anakim, who appeared to grow, to soften, to return to youth.

Through a smoky haze this specter became a figure whose head came near to touching the ceiling of the Temple – whose face glowed as if from an inner light, whose eyes were *indistinct* ... and then suddenly David felt his body go slack, and he was tilting backwards – though only in his thoughts, as his entire body felt unnaturally stiff.

In his mind's eye he passed into the earth and was now in *darkness*, though he knew that far above him remained the Anakim in the Temple, while above him in *another* direction he sensed Eliab, tending to Abinadab, who apparently had taken an arrow to the ankle and was in high fever, in pain.

His mind felt like it was expanding, and he had the sensation of thousands of stalks of wheat emerging from his mind, absorbing life *from* him but returning life *to* him, and then he was a *stalk* of wheat, and felt a chasm between him and every other of his kind – he was filled with such loneliness and fear that he wanted to strike into a run.

And then Ozem was standing over him as he sat in the middle of the field and said, "Wheat doesn't *run*, David," and David asked, "Is it *over*? Did the ritual *end*? Where *are* we?"

Ozem smiled and said, "You've been gone for nearly *two weeks*, David. We were beginning to get worried!"

"But I feel like there was something really important I was supposed to understand about the *wheat*," David said, turning his head to see that Michal was standing nearby, and the ridiculousness of his last statement made him feel utterly naked.

"Not about the *wheat*, exactly," Michal said, pointing at the horizon at a single sheep who stood eating grass, "That's probably a metaphor closer to your frame of reference, *shepherd*."

"Do I know what a *metaphor* is?" he asked aloud, suddenly realizing that Ozem and Michal were no longer with him.

He got to his feet and looked in all directions in alarm. The alarm dissipated when he caught eye of the *sheep*, understanding that he was meant to follow Michal's direction.

The sheep didn't stop eating as he approached, and did not react when he was moved to stroke its woolly back.

"Do *you* know what a metaphor is, little one?" he asked, and thought for a moment it might actually respond to his question.

It did let out a bleat, suddenly, and David looked up in the direction the sheep was now gazing. Standing fifty yards from them he saw a large wolf – and he realized that it was larger than *him*, had snow white fur that glowed faintly, and he could visualize the wolf taking the sheep in his mouth and rending the flesh, tearing, blood spraying in all directions, and he went *dizzy* from concern for the safety of his charge. And it *was* his charge, *his* responsibility – for this sheep could not defend itself, could not escape pursuit, and there was nothing else in the universe who would care for this sheep.

This wolf will not get within *ten yards* of this sheep, he thought. This sheep will *not* vacate his bowels in fear and bleat in terror. He strode off towards the wolf, who had taken to pacing back and forth, contemplating whether or not to come after David.

"What do you think he's seeing?" Talmai asked Goliath as he sat down on a bench and warmed his hands. They both were regarding David, who sat nearly rigid as a tree, his hands slumped at his sides, eyes closed.

"What did *you* see?" Goliath asked with a toothy grin, throwing a small log onto the fire.

Chapter 24

As the mountain continued to tremble, a harsh wind began to blow through Eden, causing Eve and Adam to shiver.

"Wait here!" Lucifer shouted, his mind abuzz with emotion and confusion and sensations he had never in centuries experienced. This included a feeling of great trepidation about entering a conversation with Yahweh and Baal.

Throughout his existence he had *never* approached the Trees with such hesitation, but he understood in this moment that he was *not* the arms of Yahweh, *not* the legs of Baal, but something different. *Independent*, the word entered his mind, as if with Adam's assistance.

He strode into the lake, and the water was nearly up to his waist by the time he had reached the base of Yahweh. He embraced the Tree – afraid, but ready to face the consequences of everything that had happened since he initially padded on four feet into the camp of the humans.

He let his mind go empty, and waited for his mind to be filled with colors and sensations and commands. *Nothing at all* flooded into him. He tightened his grip on the bark of the Tree as if to *squeeze* words out of the Tree, but there was nothing forthcoming, and he stepped back, reeling from the implications.

"Adam, Eve," he said as he slogged his way back to the edge of the lake, "I think it is a good idea for us to leave this place now. I will try to communicate directly with Baal, but …"

Above him he looked to the lip of the valley of Eden and saw a huge ape Nephilim, swinging from the branches of a tree. Two hundred yards to the left of the faintly glowing ape, past the waterfall into the valley, he saw an elephant Nephilim. He could only vaguely discern their thoughts, and what he discerned began to worry him greatly.

All doubt soon vanished from his mind, and he strode past Eve and fell to one knee in front of Adam.

"I need you to listen to me very carefully, Adam," he said. There was a violent explosion of thunder from the top of the mountain next to the valley, and Lucifer looked up to see smoke pouring out of the top of that mountain, which was a new sight to his eyes.

"Whatever you're *thinking* now, *feeling* now – you have to *bury* it inside and work through it later," he said, "You are to *protect* this woman – she is not quite recovered from injury and will find it difficult to walk, but you *must* get her back to your people. I'm not sure all of the Nephilim will want you to make it to your people, though I'm quite sure their first concern is to expel you from this Garden … it is *forbidden* for you to be here any longer, of *that* I am certain …"

With that, Lucifer strode past Adam and made his way up the incline to the top of the canyon. Adam saw lightning stream across the sky, saw wind blow the canopy of the huge Tree next to him, causing stray leaves and twigs and an apple or two to drop at Eve's feet.

He resolved to do exactly as Lucifer had just ordered him to do. He would bring Eve back to their sons, safe and sound, and *nothing* on the Earth would prevent him from doing so.

Eve had made her way to Adam, taking his left hand with her right hand and saying, "Adam, *husband*, I am sorry to have left our tribe the way I did – I was filled with a curiosity I cannot describe – there is so *much* I have to tell you."

Adam looked at her with eyes full of hurt and said, "We will talk about it later."

Adam still found the notion of talking a bit novel, conversation being something at which he was not adept, and had only engaged in sincerely since the coming of the Nephilim.

But now, talking felt inevitable. Talking and *naming* and trying in earnest to understand the world in which their tribe lived.

He took her hand and began directing her up the incline to the top of the valley. She limped slightly, wondering how it was possible her left ankle could support any weight at all, given how it had felt before.

Lucifer had made his way to the base of Baal, whose branches were also being buffeted by strong wind, rocks tumbling at his feet as the mountain continued to tremble. He knelt down and turned to sit next to the Tree.

As he emptied his mind, he felt a tornado of information enter the emptiness, and he gasped loudly, his head rolling back from the onslaught. He could feel a sheen of sweat sprout on his forehead and was acutely aware of the sensation of having a stomach half full of apples being *digested*.

Adam and Eve turned to look at Lucifer and both were filled with nameless dread. Far above Lucifer they saw smoke pouring out of the mountain and mingling with dark clouds that were folding and unfolding in chaotic patterns. They felt like frightened, awestruck children, and – *BOOM* – there was thunder to complete the sensation.

Adam turned to his left and urged Eve away from the direction of Baal and Lucifer. He gazed ahead at the path before them and his eyes locked on the humongous glowing, swinging ape, not knowing if the ape would hurt them or simply push them away from the Valley.

Lucifer was flung from Baal, landing unceremoniously in a pile at the edge of the canyon. He vaguely wondered whether or not he would awaken with repaired body as he had before, were he to have fallen over the edge onto the rocks below.

He looked up to see Adam and Eve had begun their way around the top of the canyon, warily eyeing the ape that had jumped to the ground near the edge of the waterfall, near where they had entered the center of Eden. Ending their collective suspense, the large ape began running in the direction of Adam and Eve.

For the first time in his form as human, Lucifer broke into a run himself. Adam began assembling a collection of rocks at his feet – there was nowhere to hide Eve except behind him.

She would join him at using the rocks to fend off the ape – and contemplated how they might seek to drive the ape towards the edge of the canyon – *over*, if possible. It was Adam who launched the first rock at the fast-approaching ape, hitting it square in the forehead, definitely slowing its forward progress, causing it momentarily to stop running.

"Eve, Adam," Lucifer said breathlessly as he arrived to their rear, "I will not allow this ape to harm you. I will do my best to keep everything in this valley from pursuing you … and you must *promise* me that you will *not* return here. It is *forbidden* – *all* of your tribe – they must *never* come here again, or the protectors of this valley will *kill* them, make no mistake."

"I have no intention of returning," Adam said, "It was difficult to come here on foot – I understood with every step that I was not *meant* to come here …"

The ape howled at them, rubbing its forehead with one of its gigantic, glowing paws. Its eyes were locked on Lucifer's, and it had a clear sense of what was going to happen. Lucifer inserted himself between the ape and Adam and Eve as they slowly made their way up the side of the foothill.

"It is worse than I ever could have imagined it," Lucifer said, "Yahweh would not even *acknowledge* me. Baal was *angry* with me, but I think he ultimately understood everything that happened here …"

Eve blushed a little, and Adam just let the words pass through his head, not allowing them to find purchase in the present moment. The wind continued to strew leaves and dirt at them, and the sky felt pregnant with rain.

"It was the closest I've ever come to hearing *words* in my mind when communing with Baal … I believe that they have come to disagree on the direction that … *everything* … is going," Lucifer shouted above the noise, accompanying Adam and Eve to the other side of the path from the ape, which was hooting and growling in a menacing tone at the three of them.

"Yahweh appears to believe that authority can only come from *distance*, and Baal favors a *different* approach … Baal more than Yahweh initiated my initial contact with your tribe … I have come to believe that I can better protect what I *understand* – and that *distance* does not give me understanding …"

It was at this moment that the ape charged at Lucifer, and he just shouted, "*GO!*"

The ape sped atop knuckles and heels, and nearly circumvented Lucifer entirely, but Lucifer grabbed the left arm of the ape and halted its progress. Adam and Eve were loping off at as fast a pace as Eve could manage, and a heavy rain began to fall on them all.

They looked back from the entrance through which both of them singly first saw

Eden … and now took their last look at Eden.

There was red-hot fire at the top of the mountain barely visible through smoke. Through a haze of rain they saw Lucifer fall, bringing the ape with him over the edge of the canyon, dropping through a throng of branches presumably into the lake below.

As they exited Eden, they both felt keenly that they would ever see Lucifer again.

Chapter 25

Twenty minutes had gone by since Marid had been met at the door by Laith al-Khaled, who had worn a striped bathrobe, and indeed appeared through binoculars from a distance not to have retired yet that night.

Marid had phoned from the truck, and had said that he'd had some news concerning the feed from Baghdad – and it was *imperative* that he stop by – he was ten minutes away.

Laith had assented. Ideally, Marid by now would have already seen the original copy of the Anakim wardrobe malfunction, and would have applied the demagnetizing device to the videotape.

Calvin and Bill remained in the cab of the truck while Javan and Lemuel and five other Homikim remained in the back. Mamoud was presumably still performing reconnaissance. Everyone was unbuckled, but tense and alert.

No one spoke. Cyrus and Dalil, the two Doha policemen, held up the corners of the black curtain and listened attentively for a signaled rap to come from Mamoud upon his return.

At the twenty-five minute mark, Javan elected to check in with Mount Carmel. As he withdrew his communication device from his vest, he felt no subtle vibration of response, saw no additional light enter the cargo bay.

This was a tell to a user *by design* that none of the beacons emerging from the device had gotten responses for several minutes. His hand froze, and he let the device drop into his pocket, eyes scanning rapidly each Homikim that remained with them.

His left hand shot out to grab Lemuel's right, which had dangled awkwardly while Lemuel mulled over how soon they might be able to grab a quick nap before heading home. The unexpected warmth caused Lemuel to arch his back and become fully alert, which in turn caused the five other men in the bay to do the same, all turning to the two giants on either side of the aperture.

Javan used the fingers of his right hand to press, stroke, squeeze Lemuel's palm, fingers, wrist, in a series of movements that kept the attention of everyone in the cargo bay.

Thousands of years earlier, no more than one tenth of one percent of an underground Anakim city would be lit by fire or by other means, and never continuously. The majority of the giants who remained underground instead of living in cities near their human cousins lived lives in pitch black dark.

Communicating by touch had developed among the oldest giants, some whose eyes and ears and vocal cords had succumbed to the rigors of the environment, and it had spread to younger generations first as a novelty, then later as a simple means of secrecy.

Although there were and always would be regional variations, sensory *dialects*, a canonical language of touch had solidified a full millennium before the Sumerian library in Nippur had been established, filled at the time with tablets containing the works of both human and Anakim scribes.

Danger, obvious.

Lemuel pulled his hands back instinctively, immediately embarrassed by his lack of discipline. Reached back out.

What we/I? Lemuel effected against Javan's wrist in a half-second, extending his hands to the space between Javan and him.

Check talk box. Living? Dead?

Lemuel reached into his pocket with his free hand and squeezed, feeling no vibration, and no light emerged into the bay. No further response was necessary.

Bill lowered his binoculars, the hair on the back of his neck having sprung to attention, unaware of the actions of the Anakim.

He turned to Calvin, finding Calvin craning his neck to look through the aperture, wondering at the sudden movement of the two giants who sat on either side of the aperture. Bill's brow furrowed, and with some hesitation, he turned back to keep eyes on the house.

Grab cloth when leave. Get everyone leave.

When?

"I see movement on the second floor," came a whisper from Bill in the cab, though the aperture into the bay.

This was followed by a grunt, and by a muted clack of hard rubber against glass.

Two seconds later, Lemuel ripped his right hand out of Javan's loose grasp and swatted near his lower neck.

Unthinking, Javan slipped off his seat, dropped to his right, away from the aperture, and he heard the keen whistle of a projectile miss his ear by less than a centimeter. A dart embedded itself into Ali's forehead, and Ali almost immediately went slack.

Javan yelled "EVERYONE GET OUT! *NOW!*" as he watched Lemuel blink in confusion, attempting to rise to his feet, slumping back onto his chair, nearly spilling to the floor.

The nose of a dart gun penetrated the aperture and fired off a second dart into Lemuel's neck.

As Javan heard the rapid sliding of the back door and pre-dawn light entered the cargo bay, his right arm swung wildly, fast as lightning, and he thrust his palm against the side of the gun, pressing it against the side of the aperture.

Calvin's attempt to pull the gun back was too slow to prevent Javan from wrapping three fingers about the barrel and about the trigger, checking its withdrawal, as well as keeping Calvin's hand locked in place.

Javan ignored the sounds of departing Homikim, yanking at the gun and pulling it four inches through the opening.

It was sufficient for Javan to thrust his left palm at the catch of the sliding panel. Just as the curtains closed in the back of the bay, the panel slammed nearly shut briskly and to great effect, as the trigger was pinned to the side of the aperture with such great force, the scream that came from Calvin indicated that Javan had successfully broken the finger.

Even if the gun was undamaged, that finger would not be able to pull the trigger again before Javan had quit the truck. He gave a split second to fret about leaving Lemuel behind, then stuffed that impulse into a recess he wouldn't make accessible until the immediate danger had passed.

As his feet propelled him past unoccupied seats to the curtain and through them, though the open door, he marveled to find that he had had the presence of mind to grab the bag that had sat at his feet. This bag contained the same type of burqa he had told Lemuel to grab, but it also contained a firearm he would soon use to do more serious harm to Calvin.

Javan landed on the asphalt of the street, taking in his surroundings as quickly as he could.

Though the street was devoid of activity, he immediately saw under a dim streetlight that four bodies lay sprawled out on the ground, ranging from eight feet to his left, to Dalil, who had made it twenty feet away from the truck.

As his mind raced to formulate a plan for taking on Calvin, as he turned to listen for the sound of the door, or of footsteps around the side of the truck, he felt a dart strike him in the chest.

Mamoud emerged between shrubbery ten feet away, holding a dart gun, and Javan dropped his bag.

As he scrambled for his bag with his suddenly-leaden right hand, thudding downward hard onto his right knee, he heard Mamoud softly say, "I'm sorry."

He didn't even the feel the second dart penetrate his skin.

Chapter 26

As soon as David entered the tent, he was embraced by his oldest brother, Eliab, who crushed David to his chest and then thrust him two feet away so he could look up and down David's body, expecting to see appendages missing, or damaged beyond repair.

Though David's face remained bruised and his right arm laced with cuts, he appeared to be intact.

An injured Abinadab and Shammah had joined them at the entrance to the tent, and now all were locked in an embrace.

"Father came here to Saul's camp to relay news of the attack on our homestead …" Eliab said, suddenly appearing crestfallen, "They took our *entire* flock, David. Thank *Yahweh* they left our sisters and Jesse unmolested after what they did to poor Raddai …

"But the sheep were led away and we have next to *nothing* now … yet you are *alive*! And Ozem? Behind you? *Ozem!*" At this, David's face fell, and his brothers as one recoiled in alarm.

"No, *wait*! He's alive, I'm *sure* of it … and I think that ultimately he will be returned to us unharmed, as *I* was …" David said, and his brothers visibly relaxed, though looks of horror became looks of confusion, and he knew he needed to begin explaining things.

"Ozem and I were taken into Sokoh, as you probably suspected," he said, "Once there, I was taken by an Anakim to their Temple of Life … and I *really* can't explain that conversation and do it any justice … but I want you to know that there's a *plan*.

"We won't be fighting the Philistines for very long. They do not intend to stay in Sokoh."

Everyone in the tent focused on the four brothers. Abner and Jonathon had come up to join the conversation.

"Are you *quite* serious?" Abner asked, "Are we meant to believe that the Philistines told you this valuable information and then let you *escape* with it? To lull us into a false sense of security?

"*Surely* you wouldn't be alive here talking to us about this plan unless it was trickery of some kind … do you not think, Jonathon? Eliab?"

"It was *not* the Philistines who told me this," David replied, "But rather two Anakim – Goliath and Talmai. Who, I might add, have *promised* me they will protect Ozem."

Abinadab had stepped back from David and looked at him as if he had been out in the sun without water for far too long.

"David, brother, I love you dearly and am glad you are alive," Abinadab said, "But if you could *hear* yourself right now …"

And David endeavored to do *just* that – and perhaps his Walk through the Fire had been recent enough that his mind had retained some facility for exiting his *usual* frame of reference, and he *knew* in a flash that what Abinadab was saying was true, and that for the sake of Ozem and the future of Israel … and *yes*, for the Philistines as well, he needed to remain quiet for a while and let his brothers take his exuberant, improbable speech as artifacts of one too many recent cracks on his noggin.

"Is Father here in this camp?" David asked, "I should really see him."

They readily agreed that this was true.

Jonathon took his turn and embraced David for a full twenty seconds before they left the tent, standing back to regard him as completely as Eliab initially had.

Ten minutes later, they were allowed into the tent of Saul, where Jesse had taken his usual seat, looking particularly pale in the weak firelight. Jesse stood up and unashamedly embraced his youngest son, hands on his cheeks as he stepped back with tears welling up in his eyes.

"David! *David!*" he cried with joy, "It's been over a day since they took you and Ozem … I had almost lost hope of seeing you again …"

David told his father about Ozem, taking a slightly different tack than he had with his brothers.

Saul assured Jesse that when they met the Philistines in battle the next day they would take prisoners, and Jesse would see Ozem again. Saul called Jonathon and Abner over to his table to discuss plans, and Jesse left with his sons to reunite with the rest of the family.

Before they had taken a step to go outside, a young boy of twelve burst into the tent unceremoniously, shouting, "King Saul! There is a messenger from the Philistines here for you! Nezzar and Matthew are with him … shall they send him in?"

"Yes, Micai … send the messenger in … and Jesse, would you mind staying for this?" asked Saul, and Jesse and his sons moved to the side of the tent. David had good intelligence as to what the messenger would say.

The messenger came in with greetings from the Philistines, and an offer to resolve the conflict between them, which had so far claimed the lives of twenty-seven Israelites and over thirty Philistine men. Saul bade him to speak freely.

"Tomorrow morning at dawn," he said, "Send your greatest warrior to the entrance of Sokoh. If your warrior can best our warrior, the city of Sokoh will be yours, and the Philistines will withdraw to Jerusalem. If not, then the Israelites must agree to withdraw to Bethlehem and further south, and not return for at least one year."

Saul stared deeply into the eyes of the Philistine messenger, nodding slowly at first, then with resolution.

"It is agreed," Saul said, "Tell your leaders we will meet them outside of Sokoh at dawn."

With that, the messenger was escorted by Nezzar and Matthew to the edge of the camp and allowed to return to Sokoh. In the meantime, Saul had turned to Jesse to discuss this potential for a quick resolution to the conflict, a resolution that would mean losing fewer men to spears and arrows.

"Whom shall we send?" Saul asked the assemblage in his tent.

"With all due respect, sir," said David, speaking quickly and speaking first.

"You should send a *lionkiller* …"

Chapter 27

Adam and Eve made their way slowly south from Eden.

Still in shock from the sight of Lucifer's fall, they could just make out a distant trumpeting amidst the rainfall, turning to see in the distance the glowing trunk of a humongous elephant just above a panoply of trees, a quarter mile behind them.

The trumpeting continued for some time, growing ever more distant. This seemed a clear message of goodbye and 'no trespassing', and Adam and Eve continued walking.

"That's an *elephant*," Adam said, though neither of them had ever seen one before that day, nor would they again in their lifetimes.

Eve smiled at the sound of the word, wrapping her arm around Adam's, leaning heavily on him as she walked with stiffness. They strode silently for an hour before the quaking Earth behind them could no longer be felt nor heard, and the rain had now become mere drizzle.

"I'm with child," Eve said as they watched the sun start to set in the west. Adam stopped walking and turned to his wife.

With every step he had taken away from Eden, his thoughts had become more orderly, and he increasingly mastered the anger that he'd needed to fight the disinclination to walk to Eden in the first place.

The picture he had in his mind of intertwined Trees so beautiful he had *wept* at the sight of them was already disappearing into the fog of a dream.

Adam now swelled with thoughts of Cain and Abel, playing tag and swimming with his sons, and he could not help but smile, much as he felt some pain in his breast looking at Eve and feeling somehow that she had *betrayed* him, though not understanding the particulars other than her departure from their camp.

She returned his smile as he laid his hand on her stomach, kneeling down to embrace her tenderly, setting his cheek against her abdomen. He stood up and took her hand, and they continued their saunter along the river, which eventually brought them back to the camp.

Adam and Eve were welcomed back with much excitement, both by their brethren and by the Nephilim, which seemed to have no awareness concerning the events in Eden, so they did not volunteer any account of their travels.

It wasn't for several days before Eve had the courage to ask Michael why they had remained with them and for how long they would stay – *when* were they to return to Eden?

Michael told them that they were only to leave if *summoned*, that they were meant to watch over the humans and protect them, to teach them and to learn from them.

A week passed in their camp – several hundred humans in the tribe of Jophet and five Nephilim – and one day Jophet felt as strongly as he had when starting the journey north that he was meant to lead his people back *south*, and no one questioned this when he made orders to break camp.

There were other women that spent idle evenings with the charismatic Nephilim – after the tribe would establish a new camp – which preceded moonlit dalliances with their husbands or with their pledged, followed by a flutter and a quickening in their wombs.

Nine months after Eve saw Eden, she gave birth to Seth.

She had never stopped thinking about Lucifer, and had not once given up the hope he would rejoin the tribe.

She had expected that her belly would swell to twice the size that it had when Cain had emerged from her, but Seth was no larger than Cain on his first day in the world. It was only in the months after his birth that Seth's growth was seen to be unusual.

Other children born in the months after exhibited the same unprecedented growth, and human children began playing with these new children, whom Adam called the *Anakim* – whose grandson would become known as Anak as a result of this naming.

To his credit, Adam never revisited the subject of betrayal with Eve – their memories of Eden were indistinct by then, and Adam felt that it was a mark of strength that he be a good father to Seth and a good husband to Eve, and he was both these things for the remainder of his days on Earth.

As you know, Seth found his way back to Eden first while still in his youth.

Many decades later – after his final conversation with Ada – Seth made his way one last time to Eden, following the map he had fashioned and painted alongside Abel.

He sought Yahweh and Baal, but in his heart knew he would trade success if instead he would descend into the valley and come upon the wizened, soft grin of his beloved older brother Cain, and he wept with bitter longing as he emerged from the forest and stood on a ridge at the base of a small mountain he recognized, with a familiar lake below him.

There was no sign of the Nephilim, whose appearances had long since faded in his mind, though he tenaciously held on to what he could remember of any time spent at their side.

He saw no sign of the Trees. No sign of intertwined limbs and roots, hosting silent debates over the meaning of caretaking, over whether a caretaker must remain above his or her charge, must walk alongside his or her charge, or must determine a reasonable compromise between the two approaches.

Seth sat on the ledge for hours, watching the passage of the full moon across the sky through intermittent veils of tears.

Chapter 28

Lemuel felt as though a sack of potatoes had been suspended above his head and, as he acted to move out from under it, he had been hit by an ice cream truck.

His arms felt as though he had just completed three hundred push-ups, and his stomach felt as if he'd followed that up by eating two thirds of a roast pig to celebrate. As mental images converged with his sense of smell and gastric system distress, he turned to his right and vomited, unsure whether in his current position this was a good move or a bad move.

As he emptied the contents of his stomach onto his right arm and presumably the floor beyond, he made an attempt to lift that arm, finding it shackled to the side of the bed in which he was currently lying. His face scrunched up in confusion and he found it impossible to shake himself into alertness.

"That's not going to help you get the chemicals out of your system," came a voice from beyond his feet, fifteen feet from his ears. "We didn't shove pills down your throats to make you feel this way."

Lemuel recalled being hit by darts that had flooded his muscles and blood with relaxants and tranquilizers, then perceived his right arm to be pinned *more* securely at his wrist and lower forearm, disallowing him from making any move that might have dislodged an IV currently feeding the blood vessels in his right hand.

"Javan, you've been conscious for over five minutes, so there's no need for you to keep your eyes closed to assess the situation any longer," the voice said, as footsteps echoed along the floor, and the odor of the former contents of Lemuel's stomach were noted by all present. "I'm quite happy to *tell* you what the situation is."

"Why don't you do that, Marid?" Javan said weakly from somewhere to Lemuel's right side. Javan did open his eyes then, confirming through glazed eyes the mechanisms of his confinement, and confirming that his sense of sight was yet another one of the five currently being distorted by whatever drugs were swimming around in his vast bloodstream.

"You're inside the house of Laith al-Khaled – that *is* his name, but he does *not* work at Al Jazeera Headquarters. I did my best to ensure that my office looked to belong to him – you no doubt made note of the nameplate and perhaps glanced at some of the papers I'd spread out on the desk," Marid said.

"Let me guess," Javan said, in slightly slurred Arabic, "He's Homikim as well …"

Marid smiled at this and chuckled a little. "You have *impeccable* detective skills," Marid said, "And it must have driven you crazy that this mission did not feel – *right* – to you, yes? When did you first suspect?"

Javan felt no need respond to this question. Lemuel lolled his head trying to get a better look at Javan, but it was difficult.

"Well, I suspected the dosage of sodium pentothal and other mood enhancers would not be enough to induce you to be *completely* chatty – no matter," Marid said.

"You are drugging us," Lemuel said through heavy lips, taking great effort to enunciate each consonant.

"We are *drugging* you," Marid said.

"The Anakim have a well-documented history of using drugs … for ceremonies … for keeping your precious existence secret … You care *so* much about humans – perhaps if you could simply *dull* us all into compliant comas your mission would be fulfilled?"

"It's the *least* we can do for you bastards," Javan said through gritted teeth, having already adopted the tack of being as abrasive as possible. Whatever it took to get him talking to the one who gave the orders rather than to this Marid, he would try.

Marid flushed, and his next intake of breath betrayed anger.

"You *arrogant* pricks. You have no *idea* how long I have waited … how *patient* I have been …" he said with clenched jaw.

"*Tell* me, Lemuel. Are the endless debates in Shangri-La continuing? Sixty *years* ... and are you *any* closer to figuring out what to do with the world Oppenheimer and Einstein brought us into?"

Lemuel had less success in masking his feelings and words, and he found that keeping his mouth closed after being asked a direct question was making him slightly nauseated.

"Yes, councils and collectives meet nearly every day, *still*," Lemuel said, "I do not have time to sift through the transcripts of deliberations, but I read what summaries I can, and try to keep up with scientific advances ..."

"I gather from the tone of your voice that you think our deliberations are worthless," Javan interjected. "Did you say you Walked through the Fire in Alpenheim?"

Marid disappeared from their limited view and whispered into an intercom at the back of the room.

The only light was provided by medical monitors and devices, along with emergency flood lights set above two exit doors, on either side of the feet of the Anakim. This lack of light suggested a basement room. The equipment that confined them was clearly custom designed and was put together by knowledgeable humans ... perhaps of Anakim construction?

"Adolf Hitler would have envied your abilities to proselytize and shoehorn propaganda into the brains of children ... told they are *special* among all the peoples of the Earth, and that they will learn all about it when they return underground a decade hence," Marid said. Behind him, one of the two side doors opened.

A white-haired short man wearing the uniform of a custodian entered. An unnerving shriek pinched through his esophagus, and his pail fell hard to the ground but did not tip over.

Javan caught a hint of snideness on Marid's face, nestling a low flame burgeoning within Javan's breast. Marid shot a cross directive glance to the man to proceed, then walked to Javan's bed.

"By the way, on behalf of *humanity*, thank you *so much* for protecting us from

Adolf Hitler. You really proved the effectiveness of your deliberations … Did you read the monthly reports on *that* petty human conflict in Europe?"

The old man picked up his pail and brought his mop to a spot between the beds, and began working on the mess that lay on the floor. Lemuel could feel his hand shaking as he brought a clean rag up to Lemuel's arm and gently worked to wipe off the vomit.

The man met his eyes, and in spite of Lemuel's current altered state, Lemuel could swear he was seeing the look of a frightened man who had spent seventy years *never* having seen a giant, nor having known of the *existence* of giants – suddenly to find himself near retirement, coming upon two in a dark basement, shackled and prone.

This thought terrified Lemuel, though the terror was thankfully muted, and swiftly dissipated.

Javan fought the adrenalin pumping through his system now, his chemically-enhanced, natural urge to remain angry, while this situation called for calm and collectedness.

"We learned a long time ago that there is only so much we can do when you human beings start to raise spears and plunge them into each others' stomachs," Javan said coolly, beginning to sweat from the effort of remaining free of sweat.

"Would you please make yourself *plain*, Marid? Are you angry because we Anakim are arrogant, or because we continue to fail you? Give us a quick answer, *would you*, so we can hop the bus back to Mount Carmel?"

"Arrogant, *arrogant* motherfuckers!" Marid shouted angrily, any pretense of disguising his feelings evaporated. The stooped man had finished with his cleaning and fled the room.

"So, is there any way we can talk to someone who actually has any *power*, Marid?" Javan said dismissively. "It's obvious to Lem and me that you're just the *hired help* – and don't get me wrong, Marid – you did a *great* job, clearly, because it's *Lem and me* lying chained to these comfortable slabs of Formica. Kudos! But honestly, you're *not* the genius pulling strings here. Again, no offense, tiny man, but you're *clearly* not."

147

Lemuel burst into laughter. He simply could not help himself, for he had recalled in a second-long frame a *lifetime* of Javan's withering sarcasm.

Javan's embrace of absurdity had lightened philosophical debates during their shared Gymnasium … had lightened lectures on trigonometry when they were all of five years in age … and Lemuel started *chortling*, finding it very difficult to stop.

Marid scowled and turned his back to the two Anakim, unwilling to betray more emotion.

When Marid turned back around, he had a sober look on his face and a blankness that Javan recognized and knew worthy of *fearing*.

This was the blankness seen on faces of those who not only followed Adolf Hitler but *loved* Adolf Hitler, and chemical disinhibitors inside him were not enough to erode his disciplined lack of concern for his own person … but he had a sudden panicked *crystal* vision of Marid plunging a dagger into Lemuel's stomach – why would Marid need *both* of them? – and he inadvertently strained against his bonds, betraying in that moment his discomfort over being confined, undermining the unwarranted, grating bravado he was trying to radiate to keep Marid off balance.

Marid approached the two giants, coming up between them, standing at their waists. He did not produce a dagger from his side, but rather, a syringe.

"This is a combination of mescaline and LSD," Marid said flatly, "I want you to open your minds to *Baal*, Javan and Lemuel. I want you to open your minds to *Yahweh*, Javan and Lemuel."

Behind him the intercom crackled alive and a loud voice was carried over it. "Marid! *Desist!*"

"I want you to open your minds to the possibility that your world has *ended* and your time is *up*, Anakim."

He entered the syringe into Lemuel's IV and inserted half of the volume of liquid. He walked around Javan's legs while a lock was being fumbled with in the back of the room. The remaining contents of the syringe were emptied into Javan's IV.

As the second side door opened abruptly – as Javan was about to get a look at the face of *someone else responsible for his incarceration* – his entire vision was suffused with green, and he sunk back with a wave of ecstasy flooding through him, robbing him of the ability to trust any of his senses for the time being.

Chapter 29

It was two hours before dawn, and David had not slept a wink. He was unsure when he would sleep again and had no genuine assurance that he would *ever* sleep again. Or perhaps, he mused ... to go to sleep knowing he *would* wake up.

His mind was an absolute fog, and had there been any food in his stomach, it surely would have been expelled in the last hour.

It was with great relief that he saw a flicker of flame through the linen of his small tent, and it was with delight that he saw Shammah enter his tent. With the way things had ended hours earlier, he had been unsure Shammah would ever speak to him again, and it had grieved him terribly.

Shammah was many things to David – brother, friend, trainer, boss, comrade-in-arms, bringer of advice. The neutral look on his face meant that he was not here as his friend, and likely not here as his boss.

"You argued forcefully," Shammah said grimly, "I still cannot *believe* that Saul chose to send you against their warrior rather than Abner or Eliab or Jonathon or Hezekiah ... or *me*, for that matter."

David was absentmindedly sharpening a sword with a stone, doing a good job at making it as close to inaudible as possible. He looked up at Shammah.

"The Philistines are sending Goliath the Anakim as their champion," David said, "And I am *telling* you that I know in my heart of hearts that everything Goliath told me is true. Neither he nor the Philistines intend to win this battle. I do not entirely understand their desire to withdraw unilaterally, but it is the generals of their army that want to do it in a way that saves face ..."

Shammah looked unconvinced. David smiled his little brother smile.

"Shammah, I wish you had been there! I met an aged Anakim and he seemed *so* wise!" he said, "They even bade me partake of an initiation ceremony – well, I *asked* that they do so; I ought not bear false witness! – and if I'm successful this morning, I will tell you *everything* that happened to me! I *understand* what I must do. I know the will of *Yahweh*, brother!"

Shammah looked stunned at this proclamation, wondering again if his brother had been knocked on the head overly hard and would be touched for the rest of his days.

"If this were anyone but *you*, David ..." Shammah said, taking a moment to choose his words carefully, as he was wont to do.

"I have always doubted that anyone who truly knows the will of Yahweh has ever actually made that claim.

"I feel that the *true* followers of Yahweh ... or Baal, for that matter ... or *any* of the other gods the peoples in these lands worship and pay tribute to ... *act* on knowledge and leave words and claims to others."

"That is very cynical, brother," David said with suspicion. "Are you maintaining that no prophet claiming to speak for Yahweh has been *honest* in doing so? Are you saying that Joshua and Moses did not lead the Israelites in good faith?"

"That *does* sound cynical," Shammah agreed with a laugh. "Like I said, this kind of statement sounds different coming from *you*, David."

David put his sword down, stretching out his leg muscles, dawn seemingly racing towards them.

"I had a *vision*, Shammah," he said softly, "So many things are worthy of protection, *need* protection ... and it is the will of Yahweh and Baal for the faithful to recognize their abilities to provide leadership, guidance, and protection ... and to give it *willingly* ... I wish I could put it into words better! ... there was a *sheep* ..."

"There was a *sheep*," Shammah said with a smile, and both of them perceived another flicker of flame alongside the tent, expecting that one of their brothers was joining them.

It was Jonathon who came into the tent, and not expecting to see Shammah.

Jonathon smiled broadly at them both, but after sitting down, dark clouds covered his face.

"David, are you absolutely *sure* everything you said last night is true?" Jonathon asked, trying David's patience. It was really too late to be still asking *that* question, wasn't it?

Jonathon reached out and took David's hand.

"Just say the word and *I* will face this Goliath tomorrow," he said, "He cannot *possibly* be as tall as you say," he said.

"*Can* he?" David squeezed his friend's hand and let it go.

"I have seen the Anakim, and *believe* me," Shammah said, "They are tall and generally *big*, and if we are mistaken about how Goliath intends to treat their skirmish, he will make short work of David."

David looked peeved, raised his eyebrows, found himself speechless.

"I *beg* to differ!" he blurted.

"Silly lionkiller," Shammah said, punching David in his sore arm.

"*Look*, Jonathon – let's go back to Saul's tent and prepare the entourage. There is not a full hour before we leave for the front gate of Sokoh ..."

He duck-walked back to the opening of the tent and stared at Jonathon with the insistence of his company.

Jonathon gave David a final look up and down and joined Shammah, leaving the tent and making their way back to the center of the camp.

"I have to imagine," Shammah said with an air of innocence that was as deliberate as it was false, "that David is well aware that Saul would reward him with anything so ever he asked, were he to defeat this Goliath and bring a quick end to this conflict."

Jonathon abruptly stopped walking. "You think David is doing this for *glory*? To become a captain like Abner?" he asked.

Shammah laughed.

"In no small part, I think David is doing this to win the hand of *Michal*," he said in a low voice, taking up their walk again.

Jonathon did not follow, but rather simply stood in place, mouth agape, trying to formulate some kind of response.

Shammah returned to where Jonathon had frozen in place.

"I feel I need to be absolutely *frank*, Jonathon, because you are my *friend*, and because David is my *brother*," Shammah opened.

"He will never love you in that way."

Shammah folded his arms after stating this, somewhat surprised that the words had finally left his mouth.

Jonathon, for his part, had turned bright red in the moonlight.

"What – why do you – " he stammered. "Love me in *what* way, Shammah?"

"Love you in a way that the Law of Moses made clear was *sinful*, and *against* Yahweh," Shammah said, stepping up to a stand one foot away from Jonathon, unwilling to break eye contact and undermine this message he needed to get across.

"But that you and I *both* know is *not* sinful, but *natural*, really. Like *breathing*.

"Though sin is in the eye of the holder of the *rock*, is that not so?"

Jonathon was speechless, ears burning red hot against his head, and as logical thought departed him, he punched Shammah in the nose, sending him to the ground.

"You *DARE*!?" he hissed loudly, having the presence of mind to realize this conversation could easily be heard by occupants of the closest tents, and he walked past Shammah's reclined body, Shammah now reaching up to stanch the flow of blood cascading down his face.

Shammah stood up, still holding his nose, trailing after Jonathon, who had almost broken into a run.

"I dare because *someone* has to," Shammah said in a loud whisper, "You have *no* notion of discretion, and really seem to have *no* instinct as to how you are perceived, nor how to perceive *others*, and *their* truth …"

At this, Jonathon stopped his brisk walk, turned around, and felt his common sense returning to him as his fist began to throb insistently.

Jonathon saw a lifelong friend gingerly pressing on his nose, bleeding all over himself, and it had been *he* who had struck Shammah.

And it was the cold-water splash of suddenly seeing himself as *others* saw him, unsure how it could have taken this long for him to have *these* thoughts, for *this* to have come up … And while he was at it, *Shammah*? *Really*?

"Yahweh's beard … he's in love with *Michal* …" Jonathon said, starting to feel deep shame for hitting one of his oldest friends, "She is a treasure, Shammah, but has that boy spoken *one word* to my sister?"

"That boy is all of eighteen years of age, Jonathon," Shammah said, and needed say nothing else at that moment.

Chapter 30

Marid and the janitor returned an hour later. Predictably, the janitor had two messes to clean up this time, which he did with impeccable professionalism, then made himself scarce.

Javan had allowed himself ten minutes of free play, having never experienced mescaline before, knowing he should only let the leash out a short lead before attempting to master himself.

His training could only go so far, given the facts of chemistry and biology. It's not as if mental discipline were going to prevent him from eventually soiling himself, and he was grateful that matter had not come up yet.

Come *out*. Whatever.

Lemuel had ridden on a wave of supreme bliss for fifteen minutes, then could not remember who he was for a while. Given his immobility he concluded that he was *Baal*, and he spent many minutes pondering creation and destruction. It was a persistent itch that eventually convinced him that he was *not* Baal, but rather a creature that itched. *Lemuel*, by name.

"I trust you are both having a good trip," Marid said in English, speaking in that language for the first time since he had met the Anakim. "It is time for us *all* to go on a good trip.

"I had really wanted to spend the past hour discussing with you the Anakim vision for the human race. I wanted *you*, Lemuel, to tell me in great detail the things your race has done to hamper nuclear proliferation that pervades *in plain sight*. I think the leaders of the world would be surprised to learn how functional the majority of their battery of weapons *truly* is."

Lemuel ignored the static that played out over the surface of his eyeballs, focusing as best he could on the blob of light that most likely represented Marid.

"It's not in the best interest of the humans to possess the nuclear capability they *think* they have – and it would not be good for them to learn that they *don't* in fact possess this," Lemuel said, sweating to maintain perfect grammar. Though he found clarity within the eye of this haze. He felt he could have talked for twenty-four hours straight and not made a single grammatical error.

"Tell us about this trip," Javan said with economy, through numb gums.

Marid nodded thoughtfully.

"Believe me when I tell you that not thirty-six hours from now, you will be addressing the General Assembly of the United Nations in New York City," Marid said, letting this information sink into their wildly flagellating brainwaves.

"You mean to *expose* us," Javan said with feigned arrogance, though he was well aware he possessed a copious amount of honest, righteous arrogance. "You would not be the first to try."

Javan already understood that this would be successful. Was *intended* to be successful, and looked forward to being unimpaired enough to begin the investigation to determine *why*.

Marid smiled and chuckled. Javan spotted a group of humans in white uniforms emerging from the two doorways at the back of the room. Two men held a syringe aloft, as if staged, and both syringes were introduced into IV feeds, and Javan did not doubt that he and Lemuel would be sedated before they were to be moved, as it made no rational sense to give them a single avenue to attempt a physical escape.

Yet Javan came from a vocation that occupied tens of thousands of Anakim, directing the actions of hundreds of thousands of Homikim, and he imagined for a few seconds that Marid and his sponsors had waited *too* long to move them, allowing enough time for Javan's people to extract them. Was this an *actual wisp of hope* countering his clinical assessment of the inevitability of these unfolding events?

"I'm here to tell you with much pleasure, Javan and Lemuel, that we are already the first to *succeed*," Marid said with overwrought, adrenalin-fueled relish.

"We began broadcasting approximately two hours ago." His eyes looked up towards the ceiling, as if making note of the cameras above, then looked about the room, as if to indicate microphones surrounding them.

This came as little surprise to Javan, and he felt the slightest amount of shame when feeling some relief that it had been Lemuel who had dramatically ejected so much efflux onto his bed and onto the floor.

"Once we're en route, we will broadcast the Baghdad tape, accompanied by things we've collected over the past thirty years," Marid said, "At this very moment we are being watched, *live*, by millions of humans around the globe …

"Also by many Anakim, I am sure, and as much as *you* would like to think they will take extreme measures to prevent our journey to the United States, you probably realize that the Councils in Allegheny and Mount Carmel are determining a *better* course, since today marks a new day for the entire planet, and we will all have to get used to it."

Balloons and clouds of yellow and maroon danced in front of Lemuel's half-closed eyes, and he mouthed, "You say that millions of humans are listening to us, watching us at this very moooo -men' ?"

Marid smiled wryly and said, "They *are*, Lemuel. And I am so glad to have forced you *bastards* to invite us to your table."

"And I am so glad to have this op'tunity to tell the millons of humans out there what an ignorant *tortoisefucker* you are – I hope the CNN and Moscov TV translators get thet *riiiiiii* – " Lemuel trailed off into silence as Javan re-entered unconsciousness with a half-grin frozen on his face.

Chapter 31

Thirty Israelites stood firm four hundred yards from the front gate of Sokoh, and hundreds of soldiers stood half that distance beyond them. Eliab and Abner inspected David under first light, adjusting his leather tunic and sheath, checking his stock of ten stones, stepping away from him and nodding solemnly.

Alone, David strode out from the assemblage, and at that moment, the front gate opened to allow Goliath to exit Sokoh. Behind Goliath came Ozem.

Goliath felt uncomfortable under the weight of his armor, spear, and a sword that ran diagonally across his back in a leather sheath. The Philistine generals would barely look at him when he told them that the time had come to end the bloodshed in Sokol by sending him as their warrior, with the Anakim people taking on the shame of a loss rather than the Philistines.

The generals understood he had conspired with David to put on a convincing show that would result in Goliath's cowardly surrender, and the Philistines would let the filthy Israelites have a city designed for neither of their peoples.

Ozem was not privy to this plan, and asked meekly, "Why are they sending David to fight *you*? This is *monstrous*. Have you no sense of *honor*?"

Goliath did not meet Ozem's gaze and sighed loudly, closing his eyes to avoid rolling them overtly.

"Your brother and I have an *understanding*, Ozem. You have to trust us both, and I would like to think I may have earned some trust from you by insisting they let you go with nothing to show for it," Goliath said.

"Rihab said that they would not want the appearance that I was being kept hostage in order to secure a victory over David," Ozem said, tearing up with soreness and fatigue and anguish, "They seemed pretty certain one of my brothers would want to avenge the needless slaying of Raddai."

Goliath felt chagrin but did not show it. They were only fifty yards from David.

"Say farewell to your brother David. You can both grieve Raddai together, *tonight* … I promise you that."

Ozem looked at Goliath, his face over five feet above Ozem's, and could not find a response, but merely shook his head anticipating having to grieve for *two* brothers with his family by midday. Ozem continued walking once Goliath had halted, not looking back nor saying goodbye.

Goliath took up a stance with legs spread, stretching his arms out, moving his spear in a slow arc in a manner he knew would make good theater. Ozem walked up to David, who smiled widely at his approach, and they embraced each other warmly.

"You *can* kill him, David," Ozem said, "His skin looks no different than *our* skin, and you will *surely* be more agile than he."

David held onto Ozem's arms and gave him another smile, "Put all your fears to rest, Ozem. Go see the rest of our family and tell them I will return shortly."

Ozem could not bear to see David smile as if he had not a care in the world. He began to cry, berating himself for the weakness, and made his way towards the Israelite contingent, turning past the rising sun to take one last close look at David, who did not look back.

David stopped when he was ten yards away from Goliath. Goliath gripped his long spear in his hands and swung it in a circle in front of him. David took out the first stone from his pocket and placed it in his sling. He leisurely spun it about his head a few times, getting the feel for it, then let it dangle by his side again.

"How do you feel?" Goliath called, taking a step forward. Then another.

David began to circle slowly around Goliath to his right, trying to maintain the ten-yard distance from his foe. "How do I *feel*?" he asked.

"No one can hear us out here," Goliath said, "So *yes*, I am asking you how you feel."

"I'm feeling better now that I see Ozem returning to the family," David said, beginning to twirl his sling above his head again.

Goliath held his spear low with his left hand and high with his right hand, moving it back and forth in front of his face in an effort to anticipate the path of – and to block – any projectile launched in his direction.

He took two running steps forward as David asked, "How is Talmai?" and backpedaled slightly.

"Talmai and I will return to our people tonight, and the Anakim will have quit Judah entirely," Goliath said, then roared into the air, "I AM GOING TO DESTROY YOU, PUNY MAN!"

Involuntarily, David let fly the first stone, which careened towards Goliath's head until diverted by the spear, causing it to slice into his temple, drawing blood but causing little pain.

"Excellent, David! We need to make it look *good*!" Goliath said, putting a hand to his head and stabbing in David's direction with his spear – for effect, as he was some distance from David. He roared and began another running lunge towards David, causing David to fumble for a second stone while trying to maintain the distance from Goliath.

"I have to thank you again for what you showed me," David said loudly, though still inaudibly to the audience on both sides of the conflict. "I *know* what I have to do for my people."

"Which is what?" Goliath asked, beginning another sprint towards David.

David had begun swinging his sling again as he crouched low – this time he feinted on the penultimate swing ... followed with a swift release of a pointed rock that Goliath barely saw leave David's position before it struck him squarely in the forehead, causing him unanticipated blinding pain, immediately checking his run, causing him to lurch in confusion.

Stone number three entered the sling immediately, and David used this opportunity to increase his distance from Goliath again.

"Saul rules our people as the *fist* of Yahweh," David said, "I intend to rule our people as the *heart* of Yahweh."

Goliath felt blood trickle now from the second wound, filling his eye, stinging incredibly.

"That was a good blow, David," Goliath said somewhat weakly, head pounding, "Perhaps one more of those and it would be my *pleasure* to surrender ..."

He dizzily brought his spear back up to protect himself, turning in place as David worked his way counterclockwise around Goliath. Mental tumblers were falling in place inside his head, and through the haze of pain he fumbled with the question, "Did you say you intend to *rule* your people?

"You ... *sheep* ..." Goliath struggled to say, unable to find the verb he sought.

"You taught me about *responsibility*, Goliath," David said, swinging his sling slowly about his head, accelerating, "I Walked through the Fire, and I understand the need for *sacrifices* to be made – by *you*, by *me*, all for the greater good."

The stone exited his sling even faster than the second one had, hitting Goliath in the temple where he had already been wounded, and this time Goliath went down on one knee.

As his skull reverberated from the blow, he now understood exactly what David intended to do, and *why* David felt he needed to do it, and for a fraction of a second felt it might be the best path, but self-preservation and love flooded his brain, and he sputtered, "David, *don't*."

Guided by instinct alone, Goliath feigned immobilization, and another stone sent his way sailed past his head, just as he sprang forward with the spear. David was caught off guard, sling now stoneless, as Goliath was running towards him, clearly not intending to stop.

Goliath also surprised him by abruptly leveling the spear at his side and releasing it towards the spot at which David stood momentarily frozen.

If Goliath had been able to commit to ending David, he might have aimed the spear at David's chest and killed him. It was because his intent was simply to stop the stones from coming that David was able to pivot awkwardly and feel the spear slice along the right side of his chest, taking a good chunk of skin and a small piece of muscle with it. And still Goliath came.

"*Listen*, Goliath – I promise you I will be open to Baal, to everything you and Talmai told me …" David said quickly as he loped off, attempting to flee from the pursuing giant. Goliath had now unsheathed his sword, trying in vain to wipe blood out of his eyes with his forearm, nearly losing track of David as he sidled backwards, backwards, falling back towards Sokoh.

"Only a *hero* will be able to inherit the throne of Saul …"

David had drawn his short sword and withdrew a stone with his left hand. Goliath was roaring now, bringing his sword down blindly, plummeting into sandy dirt where David had been a second earlier.

With a quick stab to Goliath's huge midsection, David dove between Goliath's legs and emerged on the other side, producing his sling and fumbling to move sword back into sheath, move stone anew into sling.

"David, you *cannot* do this …" Goliath cried as he felt blood pour from a shallow vertical gash between the abdominal muscles at his stomach.

He whirled around in time for another stone to smash his nose, breaking bone, and he fell onto his back, unable to move his sword arm quickly enough before David was on him, stepping on Goliath's right wrist, plunging his sword into Goliath's forearm.

With every ounce of strength he could muster through the screaming agony, Goliath brought his left arm over his stomach, striking David precisely where the spear had removed a piece of David, sending him flying to Goliath's right side, tumbling end over end.

He strove now to reach David's sword, which had gone entirely through his right forearm and six inches into the soil, forcing his hand to flex and deflex involuntarily, inches from where his own sword had dropped onto the dirt.

"Goliath, I will do *right* by all of Judah, by the Philistines … I will achieve what Saul cannot, with his limited perspective. You opened my *mind*," David said, slowly walking towards Goliath, whose fingers of his left hand scrabbled in vain after the hilt of David's sword.

Goliath watched as David approached calmly. He felt very tired, in blinding pain, angry.

"David, my wife is giving *birth* soon," Goliath said through spittle and blood, "I *beg* of you not to do this."

"But you understand why I *have* to," David said. "And I *will* make amends with the Anakim."

This statement lit a fire under Goliath and he worked harder to grab David's sword, just as David picked up Goliath's. He tried to use his right leg to kick at David, who easily stepped closer to Goliath's head, out of range.

"David, the Anakim are *leaving* this world. You have *no idea* how hard it is for our women to give birth ... how *rare* it is for offspring to be born ..." Goliath choked, understanding now what was going to happen, wondering if he could do some good by following this with the right words.

To sell the lie the Anakim had put into motion a century earlier.

"David, the humans *alone* possess this world. It is up to *you* to lead the Israelites and perhaps one day *other* peoples, but you should not do this by sword alone. Be wary of any and all who claim to speak on behalf of Yahweh and Baal ... surround yourself with *wise* people, not *pious* people ..."

David looked extremely upset, but Goliath did not doubt the strength was in the boy to finish this as he had intended to before the battle had begun.

He strained to think of better words to leave the world with, words that might help others live, both Anakim and humans. In a moment of lucidity, he embraced the mission he was part of – to help the Anakim disappear from the memory of mankind.

"There are only a thousand Anakim left in the entire world, David, and most of them are as old as Talmai ..." Goliath lied. "You need *not* pursue them ... my people have almost entirely perished ..."

Goliath's own sword now plummeted down into his neck, and Goliath expired within seconds.

David staggered back and fell abruptly onto his backside, having a hard time processing what he had just done. Having come through the Fire he had emerged with a *plan*, and he knew he had just witnessed the beginning of his path to becoming a great ruler.

He sensed his brothers running towards him, and he crawled over to where Goliath lay, and gazed at the pain captured in those lifeless eyes.

Tears gushed down his cheeks and he embraced Goliath.

He looked toward Sokoh through a blur of salt and water as generals and soldiers emerged with weapons sheathed and their standard lowered, and he knew that Saul was going to meet them with Abner and twenty Israelites – to accept their formal surrender.

It took three of his brothers to pry him away from Goliath's body, and they practically carried him back to their camp, forcing him under blankets in his tent, keeping guard with Jonathon at the mouth of the tent.

It was over twenty minutes before they heard David's sobs subside, and knew that he had finally, mercifully, fallen asleep.

Chapter 32

"Do you think Seth had found the original Eden, or had he come to the wrong place?" Alisha sleepily asked Leph.

Leph had finished his long narrative after three successive evening visits. Alisha looked much improved from two days earlier, and Miriam had told them she was very likely to give birth in less than a month, and with a minimum of complications.

"I think they were *surely* in the right place," Leph said, "Though he did not find the Trees his parents had described, nor any sign of the Nephilim. Many believe that for the first time in living history Yahweh and Baal fell out of accord, and they destroyed the vessels that had sustained them for thousands upon thousands of years."

"Destroyed their vessels and went to their separate corners?" Alisha asked, taking Leph gently by the hand again.

"It's all a matter of faith at this point," Leph said, "Some people believe they departed this world forever, having found their task to protect the world *impossible* – once the world had produced reasoning beings with *thumbs*, filled with awe and hunger and need."

"Or they left their task to the Nephilim, who also seem to have quit the world, or perhaps could not truly exist without Yahweh and Baal ..." Alisha continued, having long debated these questions with Leph, with friends, with fellow students in Gymnasium, and within subsequent educational collectives.

"I feel so conflicted about the world, Leph," Alisha said wistfully, "Do you really think the humans can help us hide ourselves, hide away in our mountain cities, so we can try to protect the world from *outside* of the world?"

Leph had pursued these questions for the last century, ever since he had heard first from his bakhati that they were to withdraw from humankind.

"We have spent centuries believing that Baal had it right – how else can you help someone out of the gutter unless you are willing to kneel down into that gutter and hold out your hand?" he asked rhetorically.

"But there have been centuries of distrust and jealousy and suspicion that we Anakim want to rule over humans – and to take their gold and shiny objects from them. All the while, the prophets of seven nations – some who do not even *recognize* Baal and Yahweh – continue to preach that we are *abominations* who emerged from the very first sin, from the very first Garden …"

A clearing of the throat, then, at the entrance of Alisha's birth chamber, and they turned to see an old friend standing in the doorway, and the face of this old friend could not even begin to disguise the news he bore.

"He is not with you," Alisha said, and still Talmai could not bring himself to speak. Alisha began to cry, softly.

"How did it happen?" Leph asked his oldest and dearest friend.

"I will tell you later," Talmai said through a constricted throat. "Alisha, you are looking well … Goliath longed to be with you again, and I know it causes pain to hear that, but it would be painful for me and you alike not to relay to you his state of mind during his final three days."

"Please give me an hour to myself," Alisha said through a veil of tears, almost unable to look Talmai in the eye in saying so, "And then I would like you very much to sit here at my side and tell me and Goliath's son everything you can remember about those final three days …"

Talmai and Leph backed up, slowly, nodding slightly, taking their leave of the grieving widow.

The widow's eyes had become steel. Shiny steel.

Chapter 33

The forty-third president of the United States sat in a conference room in the basement of the White House. Four of his cabinet members watched a television broadcasting Fox News.

The feed that intelligence placed coming out of Qatar, likely Doha, had been played in its entirety twice now, including an entire hour in which what appeared to be two giant men strapped to medical beds, alternately thrashing about, moaning, and vomiting on themselves.

"In the name of galloping Christ where the *hell* is Dick?" George Walker Bush shouted, getting up to pace the room for the sixth time in the past half hour.

"*Fuck* me, Amadeus," he muttered under his breath.

To be continued in

In Those Days:
The High Places

The Anakim Chronicles Book I: Part 2

About the author:

David Perry has been working on the Anakim Chronicles novellas for the past decade, with *Through the Fire* initially brought to life the first time he participated in National Novel Writing Month (see www.nanowrimo.org).

His previous writing can be found in Blanche Knott's *Truly Tasteless Jokes X* (two dirty jokes authored at the tender age of 15), as well as *Maximal 2-Extensions with Restricted Ramification*, co-written with his thesis advisor, Nigel Boston, appearing in the *Journal of Algebra* **232**, 664–672 (2000). He also contributed nine short essays to Metro Books' *30-Second Math*, one of those books in series perennially relegated to bargain bins at Barnes & Noble, where they ideally end up as thoughtful, well-timed gifts to grandchildren.

The author grew up in Wisconsin, but for the past twenty years has lived in Baltimore. He also frequently spends summer weeks in Lancaster, PA, as an Instructor for the Johns Hopkins' Center for Talented Youth program, teaching two three-week-long courses he had the supreme pleasure of co-architecting: Cryptology and Advanced Cryptology.

He is just shy of 5'11" tall.